The Book of Smith

BOOKS BY ELSDON C. SMITH

Naming Your Baby
The Story of Our Names
Personal Names: An Annotated Bibliography
New Dictionary of American Family Names
Treasury of Name Lore
American Surnames

THE BOOK
OF
SMITH

By

Elsdon C. Smith

Illustrated by

Frank Baginski

Edited By
Stephen C. Brice

A PARAGON BOOK

To My Wife
Clare

Paragon Books
are Published by
G. P. Putnam's Sons
200 Madison Avenue
New York, New York 10016

This is an authorized reprint of a hardcover edition
published by Nellon Publishing Company, Inc.

Library of Congress Cataloging in Publication Data

Smith, Elsdon Coles, date.
  The book of Smith.

  (A Paragon book)
  Bibliography: p.
  Includes index.
  1. Smith (Name)   I. Brice, Stephen C.   II. Title.
CS2508.S6S54   1979   929.4   79-10098
ISBN 0-399-50393-5

First Paragon Printing, 1979

Printed in the United States of America

PUBLISHER'S NOTE

Even though THE BOOK OF SMITH took fifty years to compile and write, it is not the final word on The Great Name. For future editions, we invite readers to contribute any stories, anecdotes, poems, jokes or anything at all that pertains to the name of Smith. All contributions will be attributed.

Paragon Books
G. P. Putnam's Sons
200 Madison Avenue
New York, New York 10016

CONTENTS

Foreword

CERTAINLY anyone living in a country where English is spoken knows, and has as friends, people with the surame of Smith. Poor indeed is he who cannot instantly call to mind several acquaintances of this name. Among English-speaking peoples Smith is the most popular surname. Almost everyone has a strain of Smith blood in his veins.

Mark Antony Lower, an early onomatologist, in his great book, *Patronymica Britannica,* page 319, after declaring that the name of Smith requires a volume to do it anything like justice, says, "Nay, I am not quite sure that a new science to be designated *Smithology* would not prove quite as instructive as many existing *ologies*, while it would have the merit of being perhaps more amusing."

This work has been in preparation for many years. So many people have helped and made valuable suggestions that it would be impossible to name them all, so I will not even try. However, I am truly grateful for the help I have receive.

As a full understanding of the origin of the name of Smith cannot be acquired without some knowledge of the history and early importance of the smiths in the various countries, the author has at the beginning set out a synopsis of that history. For the same reason some space has been given to an account of the smith as a character in myth and legend. But the principal emphasis of the work is upon the origin and significance of the honorable name of Smith, to which is added the opinions of the sages and the poets, together with jokes about the name and all those miscellaneous, interesting, but little known facts about the Great Name.

—Elsdon C. Smith

CHAPTER 1

Smiths Are Everywhere

THERE are approximately 2,180,960 Smiths in the United States. This estimate is based on the machine count of the names of people with Social Security numbers made by the Social Security Administration of the Department of Health, Education, and Welfare. 1.0144% of the names in the Social Security Records are Smiths, so 1.0144% of the people in the United States are named Smith. One man out of every 100 is a Smith. Because of the influx of immigrants, the proportion of Smiths to the population has been gradually decreasing. In 1930 one person out of 86 was a Smith. These figures do not include the 125,900 Schmidts in the country.

Table of Estimated Number in The
United States According to Various Spellings

Smith	2,180,960
Smyth	9,600
Smythe	570
Smithe	160
Schmidt	125,900
Schmitz	24,370
Schmitt	23,900
Schmid	9,700
Schmit	2,160
Smit	870
Smitt	250
TOTAL	2,378,440

1

The Smiths could entirely populate the states of Alaska, Delaware, Vermont, and Wyoming and have more than 400,000 left over. They could more than fill any two of the following states: Hawaii, Idaho, Maine, Montana, Nevada, New Hampshire, North Dakota, Rhode Island, and South Dakota. They could entirely fill either Arkansas, Nebraska, New Mexico, Utah, or West Virginia and still have many left. In other words there are more Smiths than there are people in eighteen of our states.

The Smiths could more than populate any city in the country with the exception of New York, Chicago, and Los Angeles. Think of Philadelphia, Detroit, Houston, Baltimore, Dallas, Washington, Cleveland, Indianapolis, Milwaukee, San Francisco, San Diego, San Antonio, Boston, Memphis, St. Louis, or New Orleans with no one living in them but Smiths! Happily for the postman, at least, all the Smiths are not grouped into one city or one state.

All together in the world there are about 2,882,450 Smiths, distributed approximately as follows:

United States	2,180,960
England and Wales	512,570
Scotland	70,790
Ireland	29,960
Canada	74,170
Other countries	14,000
Total	2,882,450

IN OTHER LANGUAGES

The above figures do not include the many Schmidts, Lefevres, Herreras, Kowals, and others with foreign names meaning Smith. There are approximately 1,853,900 of these. Adding this number to the above total we reach the astounding number of 4,736,350 persons in the world who are named Smith, either in the English language or in some other language.

As the proportion of Smiths to the rest of the population varies greatly in different parts of a country, especially in the United

States, great care has been taken to avoid basing the estimate upon just one section of the country. Some writers have, for example, estimated the number of Smiths in the country as a whole by taking as a standard the proportion of Smiths in the New York City directory. That such an estimate is fallacious is almost self-evident when one remembers the percentage of foreigners in New York.

In the above estimate of Smiths and Smith names in this country numerous directories have been used, both city and trade, but in the final estimate great reliance was placed upon the proportionate number of Smiths listed in the government social security records as compared to the total population. This great group of people was picked from the country as a whole, no part of the country furnishing an undue proportion of workers although it is true that a larger proportion of city people are on the social security rolls than country people. None of the large American cities can be said to be truly representative of the country as a whole.

WHY SO MANY?

There are several reasons for the great number of Smiths. As will be shown later, the constant need for metal in war and peace and their early importance caused many metal workers to be in existence at the time when the peoples of England and the Continent started to acquire permanent surnames. Most men could do their own work in the other trades, but had to go to the smith for the metal work. Consequently there were more workers in the smith trade than in most other trades. As the smiths were respected and honored, families were glad to become known by the name of Smith.

In 1181 in England, King Henry II raised a permanent force by a law compelling every burgess or freeman to own an iron headpiece, a lance, and either a hauberk (long coat of mail), or a gambeson (leather protective garment), according to his means; this was supplemented by the addition under Henry III, in 1253, of swords and knives to the infantry equipment, and the maintenance of a reserve force composed of those persons possessed of less than forty shillings of land, who were compelled to arm themselves with scythes, long-handled axes, knives, and other rustic weapons. Such wholesale arming of the common people would naturally require many smiths. This happened just before the acquisition of surnames by the trades people and resulted in a great number of Smith families.

Some have claimed that Smiths abound because of the countless defunct compounds, such as Arrowsmith, Blacksmith, Goldsmith, Gunsmith and Silversmith. While this is true to some extent, it is not by any means the chief cause of the Smiths' popularity. In describing a man as "the Smith" it was not necessary to say that he was a silversmith or a blacksmith, so consequently the shorter term "Smith" was used and became the surname. The term *Smith* meant all workers in metal, although it did mean more specifically ironworkers. The workers in iron far outnumbered all the other smiths put together.

MACGOWAN TO SMITH

In the year 1465, in the reign of Edward IV, a statute was passed requiring every Irishman dwelling within the English pale, then comprising the counties of Dublin, Meath, Lowth, and Kildare, in Ireland, to take an English surname. In obedience to this law many Irish MacGowans translated their name to the English Smith.

But the real reason why there are so many Smiths is because there was one, and generally only one, smith in every small village community in England, and he was an important and respected citizen. Consequently he was referred to as "the smith," and in time that became his surname. Since there was only one in the village, *Smith* identified him. The smiths were never so numerous as the farmers or the fishers. But, as the farmers and fishers lived in groups, the occupational term was not a proper identification. People named Fisher come from the inland districts. It was not until a fisherman left the seaside that he would be known as Fisher.

A minor reason for the popularity of the surname of Smith is because it came from a trade, the smiths, who were notorious for their strength and general good health. Longfellow recognized this in his celebrated poem, *The Village Smith.* Smiths, being healthy, raised large, healthy families.

Thus we find that there are more Smiths in the United States, England and Scotland than any other name. There are more in proportion to the population in Scotland than anywhere else. In the last century statistics showed that one in every fifty in Edinburgh was named Smith, and one in every sixty-nine in the whole country.

The name of Smith stands fifth in Ireland. In Germany the Schmidts, under various spellings, stand first. In France the Lefevres are ninth while the Lefebvres are eleventh, and together they rank second.

GYPSY SMITH

Smith is one of the principal clans of Gypsies. Little is known of their names before they came into England in the fifteenth century, and it is probable that they had no surnames before that time. At the present day they have borrowed some of the most common English surnames.

If names were being assigned today, the Smiths would not lead because of the great change of occupations. In this machine age the importance of the individual smith has dwindled, until today he is only a shoer of horses, almost extinct even in rural districts.

When God had made man he said, "Be fruitful, and multiply, and replenish the earth, and subdue it," (*Gen.* i, 28) and repeated his injuntion to Noah and his sons (*Gen. ix, 1*). The Smiths seem to be the only group that really tried to obey the divine command. And yet it has been said that even the fall of a sparrow is noted, but there are just too many Smiths. But, "if the Smiths be for us, who can be against us?"

Smiths will be found in all English-speaking countries as it is a distinctly Anglo-Saxon name. For that reason there are more Smiths in the British Isles in proportion to the population than anywhere else. In different parts of this country the relative frequency of the name is in almost direct proportion to the ratio of English people (including the Scots, but not the Irish). Germans in this country have not reduced the relative frequency of the Smiths owing to the fact that Schmidt is such a common name in Germany. Thus the name is least numerous in New York and other Eastern cities with a large foreign-born population, and most frequently found in the South and Middle-West.

ANGLO-SAXON SMITH

In England the relative frequency of Smith varies greatly in different parts of the country. It is found least often in the three south-west counties of Cornwall, Devon, and Somerset, where, it may truly be said, the Smiths do not flourish. It is also found infrequently in Wales. Its great home is in Worcestershire and in the adjacent counties of Gloucester, Warwick, and Stafford.

Smiths are also very numerous in Essex, in the east of England. In the extreme north, it is rather less frequent; but it extends in numbers across the border, and is established over the greater part of Scotland, being most numerous in the counties south of the Forth and the Clyde. If England is divided into three parts by two lines, joining the Thames with the Severn, and the Wash with the Dee, it may be observed that the Smiths are most numerous in the middle division, less frequent in the northern division, and least numerous in the south.

In Ireland, the Smiths are found in every county, but they have been discovered in the largest numbers in Antrim, Cavan and Dublin. MacGowan (Irish form of Smith) is found chiefly in Cavan, Donegal, Down and Leitrim.

In France, the Smiths, or in the French, Lefevres and Lefebvres, are pretty evenly spread throughout the country. In Germany, however, the distribution of Schmidts is not uniform owing to the differences between High German and Low German. The spread of the High German form of the language all over Germany made the form Schmidt more common than Smidt.

The Schmidts are more numerous in the southern part, which was the original home of the High German dialect, than in the northern part or Low German district.

OTHER NAMES OTHER SMITHS

Besides the Smiths proper there are many disguised Smiths passing under other names, who are, in their origin, genuine members of this great clan. For example Forge, anciently written Atte-Forge, is a local name with the same meaning, as it is certain that the first with that name wielded the hammer.

Some Whites may derive from the Anglo-Saxon *hwita,* a smith in the sense of a sharpener, armorer, or swordsmith, rather than the Anglo-Saxon *hwit,* white.

The Wrights derive their name from their occupation, but in early times the work of the wright was included with that of the smith. In fact the wrights are an offshoot of the smiths, taking the place of the woodsmiths.

Another very common name is Marshall, which, when surnames were being acquired, meant blacksmith; also a farrier, horseleech or horse-smith. Most of the bearers of this name (and it ranks sixtieth among the common names in England) are thus descended from an ancestor who was a smith, as the military meaning of the word was not developed until a much later period. The same is true of the French name *Mareschal,* which, like the English word, is derived from the Old High German *marah-scalc,* literally horse servant.

As the term Smith was originally applied to all mechanical workmen who wielded the hammer, including the workers in wood or the carpenters, the name of Carpenter might well be classified as a related name. *Carpenter,* a French word, was not commonly used in England in the reign of Edward III. The Wycliffe translation of the New Testament proves that in the fourteenth century *Smith* and *Carpenter* were synonymous; and the latter was then newly introduced into the language.

Some would even relate the names of Brown and Black to Smith. It is said that the Browns belonged originally, perhaps, to that large class of men which cultivated the earth, or at least their ancestors must have spent much time out-doors, and thus tanned and browned by the sun's rays, they won their popular surnames. The Blacks were more tanned, and hence their name. So, they say, the Browns and Blacks belong really to the genus Smiths, for they were Smiters too.

G. R. Dolan, in his *English Ancestral Names,* a work devoted to medieval occupations, lists 66 surnames found in England referring to the smiths or workers in metal. He lists more than four hundred more who, he thinks, designated smiths who made certain metal articles such as horseshoes, shears, axes, hammers, locks, anchors, knives, weapons, and armor, or who worked in various metals.

SPELLING VARIATIONS

Taking into account the fact that several hundred years ago, when surnames came into use, spelling was at the discretion of the writer, it is remarkable that such a common name as Smith should be so consistent in its spelling. When one whose name is Smith is asked how he spells it, he knows that he is merely being asked his name in a polite way, and he generally replies, "Smith." A lot of names, which at first glance seem to be just variations in the spelling of Smith, can be accounted for on other grounds. A number of these are explained in Chapter 9. There are only a few spellings which need to be examined here.

The most common variations in the spelling of the name concern the changing of the *i* to a *y* and the adding of an *e*. Thus the names *Smyth, Smythe* and *Smithe* are the more important variations, the latter being, curiously, a very rare name.

The jibe at the Smyths for that harmless *y* in their name is always good for a laugh. A great many people seem to think that it is a modern affectation when it is almost invariably the spelling in the early rolls and literature of England.

For instance, the word is found three times in Chaucer's *Canterbury Tales.* For the spelling there reference can be had to the Chaucer Society's *A Six-Text Print of Chaucer's Canterbury Tales,* which lists the Ellesmere, Hengwrt, Cambridge, Corpus, Petworth, and Lansdowne manuscripts. In the Knight's Tale (line 2025) the spelling in the various manuscripts is as follows (the order being the same as the order of manuscripts given above): Smyth, Smyth, smyth, smith, Smyth, smithe. In the Miller's Tale (line 3761) it is:

smyth, smyth, smyth, Smyth, smyth and smythe (smyþe), and again (line 3781) it is: smyth, Smyth, smyth, smith, smyth and smyththe (smyþþe). The same writer does not always spell it the same in the same manuscript. Thus the Corpus manuscript spells it: smith, Smyth and smith.

In the very earliest writings, however, it is generally spelled with the *i*, as in *Beowulf* and the *Anglo-Saxon Chronicle*. The spelling of the name has no bearing on the age of the family.

The use of *y* as a substitute for *i* had been established by the middle of the thirteenth century. Scribes used it as a convenient means of breading up an ambiguous series of minims produced by a succession of *i, u, n, m* as *nym, myn, ynumen* for *nim, min, inumen*. This free use of *y* was continued through the Middle English period and lasted for a long time after the introduction of printing; but *i* was gradually restored to its place and Elizabethan Smyths became Victorian Smiths. In some words the *y* was retained giving us *dye* and *gypsy*. One would not think of spelling Sylvia with an *i*. Some authorities have explained the change from *i* to *y* by pointing out that many persons used the double *i* in spelling the name, especially when the *i* was pronounced long. The double *i*, as may still be seen in physicians' prescriptions, was written *ij*, a custom which led to the formation of the *j*. In writing, with the dots omitted, the *y* was easily introduced. The dot over the small *i* was originally no part of the letter, but is derived from a diacritic mark, like an acute accent, used to particularlize the *i* in positions in which it might have been taken merely for the stroke of another letter, as in *quiet*.

A curious variation, and one that seems harsh both to the eye and the ear, is *Smijth*. It has been clamed that the Mr. Smith of the 'transition' period, having substituted *y* for *i*, was so delighted, that he tried to decorate his name even more by adding a tittle to each stroke of the *y*, thus producing the *ij* of the existing *Smijth*! Others have suggested that the form comes from the ancient custom of dotting *y*. The dotted *y* had, however, only one dot, as *y*. The correct explanation is that the double *i* was substituted for the *i*, which being written *ij*, as was the custom, became naturally *Smijth*. Much ridicule has been heaped upon this name, but at least it is not a modern conceit as an important family of that name lived during the reign of Henry VIII.

The final *e* in *Smithe* and *Smythe* (when the word does not mean Smithy) is the result of a terminal flourish by the scribes. At a time when few could write and no printing was done, the devices used by the scribes had an important influence on spelling. Owing to the retention of the *e* in English words to indicate pronunciation, *Smythe* is quite common, while *Smithe* is seldom found as a modern name.

In the Devon dialect the *ee* was the equivalent of the *i*, so there a Smith is sometimes found as *Smeeth*. Even today, many people sound the *ee* in *been* as *i*. The same is true of *breeches* and *coffee*.

In regard to disguising the name of Smith by changing the spelling, the following paragraph found in *Chambers's Journal*, about the middle of the last century, is amusing.

"O rash mortal! disguise thyself as thou wilt, thou art a Smith still—pure simple undefiled, the true worshipper will ever feel thy presence; thou art still recognisable; assume any mask thou wilt, or even veil thy time-honoured features, yet thou art a Smith. Smyth, Smytjhe, Smithett, Smithies, Smithsone, Smythers, Smithurst, Smythwaite, Szhinxmydljhskikoff, Honble. Montjomery-Byron-Dudley-Fitz-Smytjhoille, Herr von Katzenellenbogen Schmidt, El

Senor Conde Don Carlos de Smitio; these and a thousand others, still are modifications, free-and-easy combinations of the prime original; its powers of adaptation to all requirements and fancies, surpass comprehension."

ANCIENT PRONUNCIATION

The available evidence points to the fact that *Smith* was pronounced in ancient times the same as it is today, i.e. with the *i* short as in *sit*, although there were provincial exceptions. The best proof of this is in early poetry where Smith is rhymed with some other word. For instance, Chaucer rhymes Smith with *styth* (or *stith*) in the *Knight's Tale*, and with *there-with* in the *Miller's Tale*. *Styth* and *with* were pronounced then the same as they are today. Spenser in *The Faerie Queene* also rhymes *Smith* with *therewith*. Still earlier than Chaucer or Spenser is *The Story of Genesis and Exodus,* an English song written about the year A.D. 1250, which rhymes *smith* with *with*. In an early English poem, found in the manuscripts in the Bodleian Library, *How þe Hali Cros was Fundin Be Seint Elaine,* goldsmith is rhymed with *with*.

Smith in early times was pronounced the same whether spelled *Smith* or *Smyth*. Today *Smythe* is often pronounced with the *y* long, as *Smyth*, especially when the final *e* is used. In England the custom now is to pronounce it *Smyth* whether there is an *e* or not, while in America *Smyth* is often pronounced the same as *Smith*. *Smijth* is pronounced *Smyth*. It is this pronunciation which calls forth the gibes in regard to the intermedial *y* in the name. A peculiar pronunciation of the name is that of Smythe, Baronet of Eshe, who pronounced his name to rhyme with scythe.

Though generally a surname, Smith is occasionally found as a first name. In the last few generations the use of surnames as first names has become common. Parents often give one of their children the maiden name of the mother as a middle name. Others are given surnames for first names as a mark of respect to some benefactor or great man.

Many men today bear the name of Smith as a first name because the maiden name of their mother was Smith. Perhaps the most famous man with Smith as a forename was Smith W.

Brookhart, former Senator from Iowa. Some years ago the
Brooklyn city directory listed a Smith Smith, a washer in a garage.
Smith Brammer Smith is from Michigan; the middle name was his
mother's maiden name. Smitha Smith was formerly listed in the San
Francisco city directory; while Smithette Smith hailed from Pittsburgh. Kovans is Magyar for Smith and Mr. Kovacs Smith lives in
New York City. A family in Southern Illinois by the name of Tribe
has attempted to give its son a name standing for millions by giving
him Smith as a forename.

There was an Old German Smido in the ninth century. We also
have names *Smithy* and *Smythia*. Thus we seem to have the three
endings, *a, i,* and *o,* so characteristic of baptismal names in early
times.

While those of the name of Smith properly enjoy the proud pre-
eminence of having the most popular of all English surnames, it must
not be forgotten that an important reason for having names is as a
means of identification. And as the surname is common, care should
be used in choosing an uncommon first name. As one writer has so
aptly remarked, John Smith is no name at all.

NAME GAME

Many Smiths have given their children distinctive first names
in an effort to set them apart from other Smiths and some have succeeded only too well, as a perusal of our large city directories will
show. Sidney Smith invented *Saba* for his eldest daughter so that she
would not have two common names. The 7th Viscount Strangford
who died in 1857 was George Augustus Frederick Percy Sydney
Smith.

Alpha and *Omega* Smith live in New Orleans, while *Major* and
Minor Smith reside in Cleveland. *Iowa* Smith lives in Columbus,
Ohio; *Missouri* Smith calls Indianapolis, Indiana his home; while *India* Smith and *Asia* Smith prefer Los Angeles. *Rome* Smith in Indianapolis, *Roman* Smith in Detroit, and *Troy* Smith in Cleveland
also belie their names.

Many little Smiths have continued in life with only a pet name
given them at birth by their parents. Such names as *Nicie, Nodie,
Sudie, Pinkie, Toosie, Birdie, Bonnie, Vonnie, Osie, Ozie, Queenie,*

Obie, Dimple and *Dovie* are found in directories. Some parents have given their children names of good qualities. We find two *Welcome* Smiths, one living in Chicago and the other in Los Angeles. *Wealthy* Smith of Chicago, *Worthy* Smith and *Joy* Smith of Cleveland, *Smiley* Smith and *True* Smith of Los Angeles, *Bright* Smith and *Pleasant* Smith of St. Louis, *Jewel* Smith of Dallas, *Early* Smith of Detroit, *Sterling* Smith of Minneapolis, *Polite* Smith of New Orleans and *Smart* Smith of Aberdeen, Scotland are examples.

Other parents have not been so fastidious. *Void* Smith is listed in the Chicago directory and *Voyd* Smith in New Orleans. St. Louis gets along with *Dub* Smith. *Sissy* Smith is in Toronto, while *Sizzy* and *Gad* Smith live in Kansas City.

People in ancient history are represented among the Smiths of today. We find *Noah, Moses, Ovid, Naomi, Euclid, Fleta, Cassius, Aurelius, Cicero,* and *Brutus* among others. In Buffalo and Toronto we have found *Christ* Smith.

Colors are *Green* Smith of Toledo and *Pink* Smith of Los Angeles. *King, Earl* and *Duke* Smith live in New York City. London is fortunate in having a *Friend* Smith.

Other odd first names of Smiths in this country are *Dotelle, Esquire, Turp, Moe, Skyring, Kibble, Lum, Bow, Creed, Holly, Dew, Young, Rush, Waive, Puck, Ome, Dock, Gain, Glee, Verde, Pocahontas, High, Orange, Ford, Urban, Ode, Marathon, Wolf, Steele, Wix, Worth, Erie, Booker, Jar, Vine, Ignatz, Toil, Chamber, Hardy, Blind, Ivory, Larn, Roach,* and *Icycle.*

Uncommon first names found are *Delphi, Elfich, Isom, Wright, Tate, Ito, Curlin, Zetta, Zillan, Zed, Jehoida, Menta, Sturgeon, Avy, Vanderbilt, Puis, Texana, Narda, Onida, Bligh, Jere, Magin, Meller, Cyetta, Celistany, Naideen, Ourel, Rezin, Trenna, Norey, Leda, Golda, Swillin, Trimble, Assip, Knea, Floy, Epuneteus, Oriarna, Vey, Bode, Murdo, Merzy, Oval, Ozell, Isola, Lexure, Euneda, Elphin, Hatsel, Aarestrup, Euler, Pola, Iber, Senath, Cletrue, Curbin, Izetta, Norva, Ola, Ona, Omer, Vonda, Virl, Zilphia, Ivul, Zeda, Zenic,* and *Zuma.*

Iphigenia, Rj, Thyge, Thyrza are not easy to pronounce, yet all these are names of Smiths in this country.

SMITH IN VARIOUS LANGUAGES

A Smith by any other name is still a Smith.

Language	Smith Form
Arabic	Khaddad
Armenian	Darbinian
Assyrian	Nappakhu
Bulgarian	Kovac
Catalan	Feffer
Cornish	Angove, Gof
Croatian	Kovac
Czech	Kovar
Cymric	Gof
Danish	Smed
Dutch	Smid, Smidt, Smit, Smed
Esthonian	Kalevi
Finnish	Rautio, Seppanen
Flemish	De Smet, De Smedt
French	Lefevre, Lefebvre, Le Fevers Ferrier, Ferron, Faure
Gaulish	Gobannitio
German	Schmidt, Schmitz, Schmitt, Schmid, Smidt
Greek	Skmiton
Gypsy	Petulengro
Hebrew	Zillai, Kharash
Hindustani	Lohar, Sumar
Icelandic	Smiðtr
Irish Gaelic	Gough, Goff
Italian	Feffaro
Kurdistan	Hasinger
Lapp	Ravdde, Smirjo
Latin	Faber
Lettish	Kalejs
Lithuanian	Kalvis
Manx	Gawn, Gawne
Magyar	Kovacs

Language	Smith Form
Neo-Latin	Smithius, Smithus
Norwegian	Smid
Persian	Ahangar
Polish	Kowal
Portuguese	Ferreiro
Rumanian	Covaciu
Russian	Kuznetzov, Koval
Sanskrit	Karmara
Scotch Gaelic	Gow
Slovak	Kovac
Spanish	Herrera
Swedish	Smed
Turkish	Temirzi
Welsh	Goff, Gowan

CHAPTER 2

The Origin Of The Name

AS *Smith* is derived from the smith trade it might be well to examine the derivation of the word *smith*, and its various meanings, as given by the leading dictionaries.

Smith is derived from the Old English, or Anglo-Saxon, *smið*, which is cognate with Old Frisian *smeth*, *smid*, (the West Frisian and East Frisian *smid*, the North Frisian *smet*, *smer*, *smas*), the Middle Dutch *smit*, *(smet)*, *smid*, (the Dutch *smid*), the Middle Low German (and Low German) *smid*, *smed*, the Old High German *smid*, *smit*, (the Middle High German *smit*, *smid*, the German *schmied*, *schmid*, obsolete.) Old Norse *smiðr*, (Icelandic *smiður*, Norwegian *smid*, Middle Swedish *smiper*, *smidher*, Swedish and Danish *smed*), Gothic *smipa*. The relationships of the stem are uncertain.

The form of smith before the twelfth century was *smið;* in the twelfth century, *smið* and *smyð;* in the thirteenth century, *smyð* and *smyþ;* in the fourteenth century, *smyp*, *smeth* and *smyth;* in the fifteenth century, *smythe*, *smyth* and *smeth;* in the sixteenth century, *smythe* and *smyth;* in the seventeenth century, *smyth* and *smith;* and in the eighteenth and nineteenth centuries, as today, *smith*.

The old explanation that the word *smith* came from the fact that he was "one who smiteth" (with the hammer), from the verb *smite*, is etymologically unsound. It has also been explained as "the smoother" (of metals, etc.), but the connection of the word with the old form *smethe* is remote, although, as elsewhere explained, the *name* of Smith is sometimes derived from the Anglo-Saxon *smethe*.

FIRST SKILLED CRAFTSMAN

The original meaning of "smith" was apparently craftsman; worker, especially a skilled worker in metal, wood or other material; artificer; maker of anything, in the same sense as our expression, builder or constructor. This general use still remains in Iceland. The name was said to have been given to all who *smote* with the hammer.

Later the troew-smith, or worker in wood, split off and became a separate trade, the wood-wright, the higher expression, *smith,* being used for a worker in metals, although it seems also to have been bestowed on a wood-wright as a ship-builder. The first requirement of a Viking was a sword, the second a shield, the third a horse, and the fourth a ship. Of these four necessities the horse is the only one found in nature. The others had to be produced by the smith who also supplied the important subsidiary wants of armor and ornament.

In time the meaning of the word *smith* narrowed down to include only the worker in metals, especially iron, and more particularly one who forged iron, a hammerman. In modern times the expression "blacksmith," a worker in iron, has absorbed the smith, the expression originating from the fact that the forged articles came from the smith, black from the forge.

The word has also been used to designate one who makes or effects anything, as illustrated by Dryden's *Hind and Panther:*

"'Tis said the Doves repented, though too late,
Become the *smiths* of their own foolish fate."

AS A NOUN, AS A VERB

Smith is also found as a verb from the Anglo-Saxon *smiðian.* As a transitive verb it means to make, construct, or fashion (a weapon, iron implement, etc.) by forging; to forge or smithy. In its intransitive form it means to work at the forge; to practice smithwork. The Oxford English Dictionary states that there is little evidence of the verb from the 15th to the 19th centuries, and that the modern instances may be derived anew from the substantive.

The name of Smith like many other famous names has given rise to a common noun, and we now find the word *Smith* used to mean the ordinary or average man, the typical citizen in this country, more particularly the name of the average man. This is especially true when the word is used with "family," as in the expression, "The Smith family." An example is the title to an article written in the December, 1930, issue of *McCall's Magazine* by Helen Christine Bennett called "Meet The Smiths of Russia." In 1944, Maxwell Slutz Stewart published, *The Smiths and Their Wartime Budget.* The dictionaries have not as yet noticed this meaning, but the use of the word in this way is widespread.

BIRTH OF SURNAMES

The working classes began to be recognized by their surnames in the thirteenth and fourteenth centuries. Trades furnished surnames because they were handed down from father to son. It cannot be said that many people consciously adopted the name of their trade or occupation as a surname, as at first only in important documents and formal matters was a surname required or used.

While it is generally known that trade names did not become fixed family names until the thirteenth and fourteenth centuries, it must be remembered that the villagers in rural England were in the habit of describing the man about whom they spoke by a reference to his trade, so really the occupational name became an additional name long before the thirteenth and fourteenth centuries when it became a fixed hereditary name.

As the smith was the most important worker in the community, it is certain that Smith was the first occupational name to be used. The smith would not resent the description of himself, and would be inclined to encourage the use of the surname.

The name of Smith is thus derived chiefly from the smith, the worker in metal. Old Verstegen, as far back as 1605, wrote:

"From whence came Smith, all be he knight or squyre,
But from the Smith, that forgeth at the fyre."

EMINENCE OF SMITH

When it is said that the man named Smith is descended from the smith, the worker in metals, it must be remembered that what is meant is not the blacksmith as we know him today, the shoer of horses and repairer of farm implements who works with very little skill, but the early English, Welsh, Irish, Scotch and German smiths, the important persons who, through their outstanding ability, were leaders in their communities. The Smiths of today are truly descended from the most able and industrious people of the community, the ones upon whom the whole country depended both in peace and in war.

Anyone might acquire the name of Brown if his complexion were dark, or the name of Jones or Williams if his grandparents had seen fit to name his father John or William. Other trade names were honorable, but did not have that same high rank that the smith enjoyed at the time surnames were being taken. Almost anyone could acquire a high-sounding place name or some momentous foreign name which might mean almost anything in the language from which it was derived. Yet many with these fine-sounding surnames of doubtful meaning affect to look down upon the man named Smith, the one who has the name of undoubted merit and most honorable origin. Perhaps they do it to detract attention from the embarrassing origin of their own names.

SMITH FROM SMOOTH

While the overwhelming majority of Smiths derive from the trade, a few are derived from the Teutonic *smeth,* meaning smooth or level. The word *smooth* in Middle English was also written *smoothe, smothe* and *smethe.* The latter form was common due to the vowel change from *o* to *oe* which was equal to *e.* It must also be observed that the name *Smith* was often spelled Smeth, due to an easy vowel change. The fact that the *word* smith is not thought to be derived from early forms of smooth does not mean that the *name* Smith is not sometimes derived from the word *smooth.* From the early form *smethe,* the English dialectal *smeeth* comes easily, and the change from that to Smith, especially in surnames, is to be expected. William Camden, writing in 1605, speaks of Smeth as a surname and defines it as, "a smooth plain field, a word usual in Norfolke and Suffolke."

The well-known Smithfield in London was at one time written *Smoothfield,* and also with the various other spellings of smooth. Smithfield was so named because of its level surface. This early spelling of Smithfield may be noted in early editions of Shakespeare. In cases where it is derived from *smooth* it would not be a trade name, but a local or place name. In some instances it would be acquired because of a personal peculiarity.

Some people were named Smith because of important incidents in their lives. English tradition has it that an early Smith family was originally Macdonald, but acquired the name of Smith, as follows: One of the family, apparently a farmer with some skill in farriery, replaced for King William III a shoe which had been lost by his horse about the time of the battle of the Boyne (July 1, 1690). The action was of sufficient importance to give the man a surname, "the Smith," which was in time adopted as the name of his family.

SMITH/FABER

A few writers have taken the position that Smith was originally *Faber* or *LeFevre*, the name being of Latin or Norman origin. For proof they point to the early rolls and other writings in which the name appears, where it is generally found as *Faber*, and claim that the name Smith did not appear until the thirteenth century, when it was then a translation of *Faber* or *LeFevre*.

This position is clearly untenable, even though it is true that the name in early times was almost invariably found in its Latin form. In Norman times when only the clergy could read or write, all the permanent documents were written in Latin, the language of the church, and the tendency was to translate everything, including the name, from the Anglo-Saxon, especially when, as was often the case, it was more a word of description or identity than a hereditary family name. Even first names were given Latin endings, as witness *Willelmus, Henricus* and *Alicia*. Later, when *Smith* became more firmly fixed as a family name, the Anglo-Saxon form is found, even in the documents written in Latin. An illustration might be noted in the Hundred Rolls of 1273. At that time a few of the family names of Smith were becoming firmly established, but most of them were more descriptive in character. Consequently the scribes generally wrote the name in its Latin form, but it is found a few times in the Anglo-Saxon form. Though the name is found in the permanent writings as *Faber*, it would not have been recognized by the common people, as they used the Anglo-Saxon language and knew nothing of Latin.

Thus, it cannot be true that many with the Latin name *Faber* translated their name into the Anglo-Saxon or English *Smith*. People just do not translate their names in wholesale lots. As for the Latin *Faber* quite the reverse is true. Most English Fabers have translated their name from the English *Smith*. During the sixteenth century scholars had a great liking for turning their names into a Latin or Greek form. However, quite a few Norman *LeFevres* have translated their name into the English *Smith,* but even they are relatively few in number compared to the great host of true Anglo-Saxon Smiths.

SCOTTISH SMITHS

Scottish Smiths have always believed that they owe their origin to the Clan Chattan. It is said that all the Smiths in Scotland are descended from Neill Cromb, third son of Murdoch, of the Clan Chattan, who flourished in the reign of William the Lion more than seven hundred years ago. Neill Cromb, a mechanical genius, became a smith and crafted various utensils of iron of great workmanship. He received his surname from his trade, and was said to be progenitor of all the Smiths in Scotland.

Many writers have repeated this nonsense about the Scottish Smiths in a serious manner. Such a statement in regard to *all* the Smiths is obviously untrue as the name originated in Scotland in a thousand places simultaneously, just as in England. Of the thirty-five coats of arms of Smith families in Scotland, only three point to descent from Clan Chattan, none of which is of great antiquity.

Other authorities agree that the Gows, or Smiths, are descended from Henry Wynd variously called Hal o' the Wynd, Henry Gow, Harry of the Wynd, and Harry Burn-the-Wind, a blacksmith nicknamed "An Gow crom," which means the crooked or bandy-legged smith. *Burn-the-wind* is an old cant term for blacksmith; *wynd* means smithy.

In 1396, thirty champions of Clan Chattan fought a similar number from another clan, probably the Clan Cameron, on the North Inch of Perth before King Robert III and his queen, visitors from France, nobles, knights, churchmen, and many common people. An inspection of the champions revealed that the Clan Chattan was minus one of their number because of sickness. A smith, Henry Wynd, offered to take his place for a French crown of gold—a great sum in those days. He was not a large man, but was a fierce fighter and an able swordsman and contributed much to the glory of the day.

It is said that as soon as he had killed his man he sat down and rested, defending himself only when attacked. When the leader asked

the reason for this, he was told by the smith that he had done his duty
and earned his wages by killing his opponent, whereupon the captain
begged him to continue and said he would be amply rewarded over
and above the stipulated wage. "An Gow crom" re-engaged in the
fight and so successful were the champions of Clan Chattan that ten
of them, including the smith, were alive, although all were wounded,
when the last surviving opponent escaped by jumping in the Tay
River.

Tradition has it that the smith accompanied the remnant of the
Clan Chattan back to their country and was adopted into their clan,
becoming the progenitor of a Smith family. This is not incredible as
Bowar, a contemporary writer though probably not an eye-witness,
wrote that the smith also bargained for maintenance for life if he sur-
vived. An interesting account of this fight is given by Sir Walter
Scott in *The Fair Maid of Perth*.

Some of the MacGowans belong to the race of Ir, or Clanna Rory,
descended from the famous warrior Conall Cearnach, or Conall the
Victorious, who was the chief of the Red Branch Knights of Ulster,
about the commencement of the Christian era, and in modern times

there are certainly Smiths in many parts of Ireland, and elsewhere, who are descended from the Milesian MacGowans.

HUMOROUS ORIGINS

In addition to the serious derivations of the name many humorous origins are also found. The story is told that Adam, after becoming very old, decided to travel. However, before setting out for the land of Adamah, he felt it was his duty to bestow distinctive names upon his descendants, now huge in number.

Accordingly, he took a seat upon a high hill and directed them all to pass in review that he might give each a fitting name. For a long time the host filed by, one by one. At last, exhausted in vocabulary,

Adam (so runs the legend) turned to the heavens with an appealing eye and cried, "O Lord, I am weary; let the rest of them be named Smith, and let thy servant depart from them in peace, for verily they are as many as the grasshoppers upon the plains of Gihon."

To those few scoffers who might be inclined to doubt the truth of this venerable story, reference might be had to *Genesis* ii, 19, which records: "And out of the ground the Lord God formed every beast of the field, and every fowl of the air; and brought them unto Adam to see what he would call them: and whatsoever Adam called every living creature, that was the name thereof."

Another facetious story has it that Cain's wife was a Smith, one of a large and important pre-Adamic family, who were all known by that name. Up to the present time no one has been able to deny authoritatively this statement.

Some people do not seem to be aware of the well-known fact that the great and formidable family of the Smiths are the direct descendants of Shem, the eldest son of Noah. It is thus derived: Shem-Shemit-Shmit-Smith. If any doubting Thomas demands further evidence, the fact might be pointed out that Shem, in the Hebrew language, means "name," and if Smith isn't a name, what is it?

Edward Bulwer Lytton, in his novel *Zanoni,* has Mergale announce a discovery he has made, "namely, that the numerous family of Smiths in England were undoubtedly the ancient priests of the Phrygian Apollo. 'For,' said he, 'was not Apollo's surname, in Phrygian, Smintheus? How clear all the ensuing corruptions of the august name—Smintheus—Smitheus—Smithe—Smith! And even now I may remark that the more ancient branches of that illustrious family, unconsciously anxious to approximate at least by a letter nearer to the true title, take a pious pleasure in writing their names Smith*e*!'"

EARLIEST SMITHS

The earliest instance of the name in anything like its present day form that the author has been able to find is mention of Willelmus Smethe found in *Pedes Finium* or Feet of Fines, for November 8, 1195. At this time the vowels *e* and *i* were sometimes used interchangeably, and the theory that this is truly a trade name is not improbable. Note that in the above Willelmus Smethe, the baptismal name is in its Latin form. Gosta Tengvik, in his *Old English Bynames* lists Ecceard Smiðt from W. de Gray Birch's edition of *Cartularum Saxonicum* (about the year 975). Of course here Smith was not really a name, but only a designation of the man's occupation.

An early instance of the Latin form *Faber,* and its origin, is in the "Chronicle of Battel Abbey," a manuscript written in the latter part of the twelfth century by a monk of the order, and now in the Cottonian Collection of Manuscripts in the British Museum. The following is from the translation by M. A. Lower:

"Among those who heard this vow, (the vow of William the Conqueror to found an Abbey on the site of the battlefield of Hastings in 1066 if he won the battle) was a monk of Marmoutier, one William, surnamed Faber, who formerly, while in the service of the duke, had obtained the name of Faber (or 'the smith') from this

circumstance:—As he was one day a-hunting with his companions, they happened to be short of arrows and thereupon had recourse for more to a neighboring smith, who proved to be unacquainted with such sort of work. William therefore seized his tools, and presently, with great ingenuity, fabricated an arrow. This man, afterwards changing his profession, betook himself to a religious life at Marmoutier, the fame of which for sanctity was then very great. And when the descent of the duke upon England was everywhere extolled, he, in order to advance the interests of his church, attached himself to the army. Immediately on hearing the duke's vow, which was exactly suited to his wishes, he proposed that the monastery should be dedicated to the blessed bishop S. Martin. The pious duke favored his suit, and benignly promised that it should be so."

Later William intrusted the erection of the Abbey to this monk, William Faber.

IN THE ROLLS

The name *Faber* is quite common in the early rolls. Several Fabers are mentioned in the Domesday book, a book which has few surnames, having been finished about the year A.D. 1086. Tenants-in-chief by the name of Aurifaber (Goldsmith) are found. In the Winton Domesday Book (circa 1128) six Fabers and two abbreviated to Faꝺ are mentioned. The Boldon Book (1183) lists four Fabers.

In the Pipe Rolls, as published by The Pipe Roll Society in England, a great many Fabers are found, one being listed in the earliest Roll printed by them in the fifth year of King Henry II (1158-1159).

In the early Fine Rolls (1199-1216) seven Fabers are mentioned as well as one Fabio, and one Fabri, the earliest of which are Ricardus Faber de Topesfelꝺ and Wulstan Fabri de Finchingfelꝺ in 1201 in Essex.

In the early Patent Rolls (1201-1216) three Fabers are noted, the earliest of which is Wlfstan Faber, 1203. In the early Close Rolls (1204-1227) twenty-six Fabers are mentioned along with one Fabri, one Favre and one Fabrica. Walterus Faber, 1207, is the earliest in the Close Rolls.

The largest collection of early surnames is that found in the *Rotuli Hundredorum* or Hundred Rolls of the date of 1273. Upon his return from Palestine, after the death of his father, Henry III, King Edward I inquired into the ownership of the lands, and of the rights and revenues of the crown, many of which had been usurped by both clergy and laity during the previous turbulent reign. As these inquiries were made upon the oath of a jury of each hundred throughout the realm, this mass of documents is appropriately known as the Hundred Rolls. Most of the surnames are in Latin, the remainder in French and English. As these are among the most valuable of the known authentic documents containing early surnames, they will be analyzed more in detail.

The following list of Smiths is found in the Hundred Rolls, the Latin abbreviations of the baptismal names being extended:

> Alicia Smeth or Smethe, Suffolk
> Nicolaus Smeth or Smethe, Suffolk
> Henricus Smethe, Suffolk
> Hugo Smeth, Oxford
> Johannes Smeth, Oxford
> Willelmus le Smeth, Oxford
> Julianus le Smithes, Oxford
> Philippus le Smethe, Huntingdon
> Willelmus Smyth, Wiltshire
> Willelmus de Smyth, Suxxes
> Magister Laurencius de Smethe, Kent

The last is probably a local name, but the next to the last is probably a trade name even though the surname is preceded by the article *de,* as the scribes were quite careless and often wrote *de* for *le.*

Other names such as *Smethefeld, Smetheton, Smethefeud, Smetham, Smythefeld, Smytheton, Smift* and *Snyth* are found. All of these, with the possible exception of the last two, are probably local names. In the Latin form the name was quite popular. Faδ, an abbreviation for Faber, led with 251, then came Faber 222, Fabr' 47, Fabri 14, Fabi 4, Fabir 1, Fabers 1, Fabian 1, Fabrie' 1.

The Norman Rolls mention Magister Petrus Smyth and Magister Thomas Smyth in the year 1417.

OTHER EARLY SMITHS

As the name of Smith became more and more used and became clearly hereditary as a surname, regardless of whether the son fol-

lowed his father's trade, it is found more and more in the English form even though the rest of the document is written in Latin. For instance, in the very earliest documents it is not found at all in its English form. Later, a few isolated instances of Smith are found and in the next few hundred years Smith almost entirely replaces Faber, even in documents written in Latin. For example, the Poll Tax of the West Riding of Yorkshire, in 1379, shows many Smiths and few Fabers.

In the "Annals of Ulster," 1171, it is noted that "Gillageimridh Mac-in-Ghaband, chief of Fir-Darcacha" died. In the "Annals of the Four Masters" we find the entry, "1341, Murtogh Mac-an-Gobhann, abbot of Clochar died."

One of the "masters of the Soldiers" (an officer chosen in Venice to replace the doges from 737 to 742) is variously called by historians Fabrizio Ziani (Fabrizio, son of John), and Giovanni Fabriziano or Fabriciazio (John, son of Fabrizio). The Fabia Gens was a powerful patrician house of ancient Rome.

A curious, early instance of the name is that found in the Petrie papyri, a discovery of Professor J. P. Mahaffy. These contain a list of names, and he says: "There is one which appears regularly in the same form, and of which we can give no further explanation. It is the name Smith—unmistakably written. We have never found anything like it before, and it is surely worth telling the many distinguished bearers of the name that there was a man known as Smith in the twentieth year of the third Ptolemy, 227 B.C., and that he was occupied in brewing beer or in selling it. Is there any other English name comparable to this in antiquity?"

The above announcement was made in the first year of the twentieth century and was soon followed by a possible explanation. The writer claimed that it is an abbreviation of Smintheus, a surname of Apollo, in which the *n* has dropped out. Whether this hurried explanation is correct or not, the fact remains that in ancient times in Egypt a man was named by a sound very similar to that of our Smith.

CHAPTER **3**

Smithereens

FIRST SMITH IN AMERICA

UNDOUBTEDLY the first Smith in America was Captain John Smith. However, he did not leave any descendants, and it was left for another to start the great Smith family in America. This was a John Smith who was born in England in 1614, and who came over in 1630. He became a founder of Barnstable and Sandwich, Mass. He married Susannah Hinckley, sister of Governor Hinckley, and had thirteen children by her—a good start.

GEOGRAPHICAL CENTER OF THE UNITED STATES

The geographical center of the United States is in the eastern part of Smith County, Kansas, the county seat of which is Smith Center. There W. E. Lee founded a Smith Center, a national capital of Smiths.

SMITH AS AN ALIAS

Smith is used as an alias more often than any other name. An interesting instance is that of Louis Phillipe, King of the French, who abdicated his throne in 1848 and fled for his life, assuming the alias of Mr. William Smith. It was he, who, upon being told at Newhaven that the name of his hostess at the snug hotel there was Mrs. Smith, remarked, "Smith, eh bien, I think I have heard that name before!"

IN THE PRESENT ENGLISH NOBILITY

Smith is the family name of the Earl of Birkenhead, Viscount Hambleden, and Barons Bicester and Colwyn. Eleven Baronets are named Smith. There are also twenty-eight Knights who are surnamed Smith.

SMITH OF NOTTINGHAM

This is a phrase which applies to conceited people who imagine that no one is good enough to compete with themselves. An old proverb runs:
> The little smith of Nottingham,
> Who doth the work that no man can.

OTHER PROVERBS

As the smith was so important in early times, it is not surprising to find a great many proverbs relating to him. They are found in many countries. Some of them, not quoted elsewhere in this book, are:

A smith's horse is aye lowin' (flaming.)
Blow smith, and you'll get money.
Like the smith's dog, so used to sparks that he'll no burn.
The smith and his penny both are black.
The smith hath always a spark in his throat.
The smith's dog sleeps at the sound of the hammer and wakes at the grinding of teeth.
The smith's mare and the cobbler's wife are always the worst shod.

Many other proverbs have been coined concerning the smith's tools. Only the most important can be given space here.

You are between the hammer and the anvil.

If you are an anvil, be patient; if you are a hammer, strike hard.

Strike the iron while it is hot.

IN FICTION

Smith is the leading character in numerous plays, short stories and novels, none particularly famous. Probably the best-known Smith character is Stephen Smith in Thomas Hardy's *A Pair of Blue Eyes*. Louis Bromfield has written a novel entitled *Mr. Smith*.

NAILS FOR THE CROSS

In *The Story of the Holy Rood* it is said that the Jews, when making the Cross upon which Jesus Christ was crucified, went to a smith to get three nails made.

> Þe iews war ful redy boune
> And ran for nales in-to þe toune;
> Vnto a smith þai come ful sone
> And bad, "belamy, biliue haue done,
> Make thre nayles stif and gude
> At nails þe prophet on þe rode";

The smith, believing Christ to be a true prophet, refused, claiming that his hand had been burned on a brand, though in reality it had not been injured. The smith's wife, a scolding woman, came out, and after abusing her husband, made the three nails.

IN LAW

In early legal illustrations the invariable character was termed J. S., initials standing, it is said, for John Smith. For example, the standard phrase showing utter impossibility was, "If J. S. returns [to London] from Rome in three days."

The John Smith rule is a rule of evidence allowing declarations of the testator as to which person he meant when there are several persons by the same name, and one is made a legatee or devisee.

THE PATRON SAINT OF THE SMITHS

St. Eloi was the patron saint of the smiths of the Middle Ages. He was a goldsmith of Limoges who became a missionary bishop at Noyon under Dagobert (640 A.D.). He died December 1, 659. St. Dunstan and St. Clement have also been called the patron saint of the smiths.

TWO ACTS

The Smith Act, also known as the Alien Registration Act of 1940, made it a criminal offense to advocate violent overthrow of the government, or to organize or be a member of any group with such a policy. After World War II, the Smith Act was used to prosecute leaders of the Communist party in America. The conviction of the parties principal leaders was sustained and the constitutionality of the "advocacy" provision upheld by the Supreme Court in 1951. However, in 1957 the court upset its position somewhat and decided that "advocacy" meant only incitement to unlawful acts.

The Smith-Connally Act, also known as War Labor Disputes Act, was passed in 1943. It gave the President the power to seize and operate privately owned factories if a strike interfered with war production.

SMITH-ON-AVON

In Shakespeare we find:
"I saw a smith stand with his hammer thus." *(King John,* Act IV, scene ii, line 193.)
"Here is now the smith's note for shoeing and ploughing irons." *(Henry IV,* Part II, Act V, scene 1, line 19.)
"I am much afeard, my lady, his mother played false with a smith." *(The Merchant of Venice,* Act 1, scene 11, line 48.)
There is a character named Smith in *Henry VI, Part II,* Act IV, scene II.

MOTHER GOOSE

Even Mother Goose paid tribute to the Smiths.

John Smith
Is John Smith within?
Yes, that he is.
Can he set a shoe?
Ay, marry, two
Here a nail, there a nail,
Tick tack, too.

THE PAIN OF SMITH

Several ailments have the name of Smith.
Smith's Dislocation of the Foot, is a dislocation upward and backward of all the metatarsal bones.
Smith's Fracture is a transverse fracture about five centimeters above the lower extremity of the radius.

Smith's Reaction for Bile Pigments is a medical test involving tincture of iodine.

Smith's Cramp is a muscular spasm of the muscles in the forearm and hand.

NO POETRY FOR SMITH

Somerset Maugham, in *A Writer's Notebook,* quotes a man named Annandale as having said, "I often think life must be quite different to a man called Smith; it can have neither poetry, nor distinction."

BAD DEAL

A Smithfield Bargain is a business deal in which the purchaser is taken in. The phrase is sometimes used to describe a marriage for money.

JAMBON SMITH

The famous Smithfield hams owe their name to one Arthur Smith, a farmer who owned the land on which the town of Smithfield, Virginia was built. Arthur himself had nothing to do with the hams. In the state of Virginia, it is in the lawbooks that no ham can be called a Smithfield ham unless it has been cured within the corporate boundaries of the town of Smithfield.

SMITH IN LIGHTS

Movies with Smith in the title include *Mr. Smith Goes to Washington; Joe Smith, American;* and *Nevada Smith.*

A few years ago an unsuccessful musical comedy played briefly on Broadway called simply *Smith.*

OTHER SMITH COLLEGES

Several colleges have been named Smith. The best known is, of course, Smith College. But there is also a William Smith College at

Geneva, New York, a small college for women established in 1908.
Then there is Johnson C. Smith University, chartered in 1867 at
Charlotte, North Carolina, and Philander Smith College, chartered
in 1877 at Little Rock, Arkansas, both of which are coeducational.

In addition, there is Paul Smith's College in Paul Smith's, New
York, which specializes in forestry and hotel management, founded
in 1946 and is also coeducational.

GERMAN SOCIETY

A contributor to Notes and Queries, of October 15, 1859, tells of a
German society in Albany, New York, in which the Smiths are so
numerous that they are distinguished by descriptive epithets and
phrases in the following manner:

> "Big Smit.
> Little Smit.
> Smit from de hill.
> Smit from de holler (hollow)
> Smit mid de store
> Smit de blacksmit.

Smit mit de pigs.
Smit mit de pig head (big head.)
Smit mit de pig feet (big feet.)
Smit mit de brick-yard.
Smit mit de junk shop.
Smit mit de bolognas.
Smit mit one eye.
Smit mit two eyes.
Smit mit de bone picker.
Smit mit two 'vrows.'
Smit mit de swill-cart.
Smit mit de segar stumps.
Smit mit peach pits.
Smit mit de whiskers.
Smit mit de red hair.
Smit mit no hair
SMIT."

GEOGRAPHICAL NAMES

Every state in the Union except Vermont and Hawaii have
honored the Smiths by naming at least a town, mountain or river
after them. In fact, most states have several places named for Smith.
The name Smith is held by 43 communities and towns, with Smiths
next at 31. After that we find Smithville 22, Smithfield 17, Smiths
Mill 10, Smithdale 6, Smithton 6, Smithtown 5, Smithland 5,
Smithboro 4, Smithburg 4, Smiths Ferry 4, Smithson 3, Smiths
Point 3, Smiths Crossing 3, Smiths Summit 2, Smith Hill 2,
Smithwick 2, Smith Lake 2, Smith Siding 2, and 22 other places in
which Smith is the first part of the name. Kansas, Mississippi, Ten-
nessee, and Texas have Smith counties, and Virginia has a Smyth
County. Other spots in this country in which Smith is part or all of
the name are: Brooks and Creeks 27; Rivers 6; Islands 7; Lakes 9;
Mountains 3; and Glacier 1. In Utah there is a Smith Canon.

Other countries have not named as many places for the Smiths,
but the following should be noted: Smithwood Common, in the south
of England (there are about 23 other communities in England named
for the Smiths); Smithborough, in Ireland; Smith Cayo, Santiago,

Cuba; Smith Channel, in Chile; Mount Smith, Smithfield and Smithwinkle Bay, in Africa; Smith Sound, in the Arctic Region; Mount F. L. Smith, Smith Cape, Smith Inlet, and Smith Island, in the Antarctic Region; Smith Falls and Smithfield, in Ontario; Fort Smith, Smith Bay and Smith Island, in Canada; Smiths Cove, in Nova Scotia; Smiths Creek, in New Brunswick; Alaska has 31 local features named after the Smiths.

In London, Great Smith Street and Little Smith Street connect with Smith Square where the headquarters of all three main British political parties are located.

Smith Street in Liege, in what is now Belgium, was occupied almost exclusively by workers in iron during the thirteenth century.

In Nottingham many smiths lived at Gridlesmith Gate, Bridlesmith Gate and Smithy Row. Goldsmith Street was not far away. Nottingham was the most famous center of the smiths in England, being known for blacksmiths, goldsmiths and silversmiths. An exhaustive list of streets named Smith or with a name compounded with Smith would fill a larger volume than this book.

Kuznetzovskaia is a town in the North Central part of European Russia. The Kisnetzky Mountains are in the southern part of Siberia.

Arrowsmith is a village having a population of 344 in the eastern part of McLean County, Illinois. Fauresmith is a town, population 2014, and district, population 26,000, of Orange Free State, South Africa, the town being founded early in 1850. It is named for the Reverend P. E. Faure and Sir Harry Smith. Goldsmith is a village of 318 in the southwestern part of Tipton County, Indiana. Goldsmith, Texas, boasts a population of 600. Goldsmith, New York, has a population of only 25 and is located in the northestern part of Franklin County while Goldsmith in Ector County, New York, has a population of 670. It is also a community in the northern part of Laramie County, Wyoming. Hammersmith is now a section of London, England. Originally it was a small Saxon village known for its smithies, called Hammerschmiede, literally Saxon for blacksmith's shop. Harrowsmith is a village in Ontario, Canada, with a population of about 400.

Besides the Ladysmith, South Africa, we mentioned in the preceding chapter, we find a Ladysmith with a population of about 3660 in the Nanaimo District, Vancouver Island, British Columbia, Canada. Ladysmith is also a community in Manitoba, Canada. Ladysmith, Wisconsin, is a city with a population of 3674 in the central part of Rusk County. Ladysmith, Virginia, has a population of 100. Macksmith is a village in the southwestern part of Lawrence County, Mississippi. Nesmith is a community in the eastern part of Cullman County, Alabama. Paul Smith's is a village of 600 in the southern part of Franklin County, New York. Schmacksmith, "A village of Moldavia's waste," is mentioned by Lord Byron in his *Don Juan.*

BRUGGLESMITH

Brugglesmith is the name of a character in a Kipling short story of the same title. The man acquires his name because of his drunken pronunciation of his address, which is Brook Green, Hammersmith, a severe contraction indeed.

CHRIST A SMITH

John Henry, Cardinal Newman, in his *Grammar of Assent,* in referring to Jesus and His disciples has the following to say: "It seems almost irreverent to speak of their temporal employments, when we are so simply accustomed to consider them in their spiritual associations; but it is profitable to remind ourselves that our Lord Himself was a sort of smith, and made ploughs and cattle-yokes."

SMITHS' CHAPEL

This chapel, dedicated to St. Andrew, was founded in the church (now Cathedral) of St. Michael at Coventry, England, by the Smiths Guild. According to Sharp's *Coventry Antiquities* the first item, in their accounts in regard to its maintenance, occurs in 1449, so it must have been founded before that date. The London *Times* of March 14, 1928, carries an appeal issued "to the scions of the 'House of Smith'" for contributions towards the restoration of this ancient chapel.

EPITAPHS

A Lancashire, England cemetery committee in the closing year of the nineteenth century took exception to the following epitaph:

> My anvil and my hammer are declined,
> My bellows, too, have lost their wind;
> My fire's extinct, my forge decayed,
> And in the dust my vice is laid.
> My coal is spent, my iron is gone,
> My last nail's driven, and my work is done.

To this the inscription upon the tomb of a West Country (England) blacksmith and churchwarden might well be added:

My fire-dried corpse lies here at rest;

My soul, well smoked, soars to be blessed.

SMITH DAY

October 28, 1905, was designated as Smith Day at the Georgia Farmers' Fair in Macon, Georgia, and every Smith was invited. The idea was promoted by George A. Smith, president of the Macon Fair Association and Bridges Smith, vice-president. An immense barbecue was served "so that the great Smith family could eat one square meal together." Hoke Smith was there seeking re-election. Buttons were given to each Smith present and prizes were awarded

for the largest Smith family, the hardest Smith to fit, the tallest Smith, the fattest Smith, the leanest Smith, the ugliest Smith, the handsomest Smith, and the prettiest Smith girl. *Smith's March* was especially composed for the occasion by Professor H. Gooding, bandmaster of the Georgia Industrial Home Band. The next day the *Atlanta Constitution* said that the attendance on Smith Day swelled to double that of any previous day of the fair.

DEDICATED TO JOHN SMITH

Mark Twain dedicated his book, *The Celebrated Jumping Frog,* as follows: "To JOHN SMITH, whom I have known in divers and sundry places about the world, and whose many and manifold virtues did always command my esteem, I dedicate this book. It is said that the man to whom a volume is dedicated, always buys a copy. If this prove true in the present instance, a princely affluence is about to burst upon THE AUTHOR."

THE TYPICAL CITIZEN

John Smith is often referred to as the typical Englishman or American. Robert Blatchford addressed his well-known book, *Merrie England,* to John Smith, taking his name as emblematic of the true-born Englishman.

PSMITH

In his book *Leave it to Psmith* by P. G. Wodehouse, the character explains the origin of his name.

"No, no, P-s-m-i-t-h. I should explain to you that I started life without the initial letter, and my father always clung ruggedly to the plain Smith. But it seemed to me that there were so many other Smiths in the world that a little variety might well be introduced. Smythe I look upon as a cowardly evasion, nor do I approve of the too prevalent custom of tacking another name on in front by means of a hyphen. So I decided to adopt the Psmith. The P, I should add for your guidance, is silent, as in phthisis, psychic, and ptarmigan. You follow me?"

IN THE AUTOGRAPH ALBUM

When autograph albums were popular the following was written by a young woman named Smith:

A friendship album is the place
For friends their name to trace,
But when one's name brings to mind
Ten thousand of his kind,
What is the use of writing it,
Or waste the ink inditing it,
A name that's meant a nation
From time present to creation?

Sorrowfully,
Smith.

P. S.—
But if I change my name,
And I'm your friend the same,
I'll add another measure,
To tell you with great pleasure,
That I am joyfully yours—

MAGAZINES

There have been several magazines published in which Smith has appeared in the title. Among these are *Smith's Magazine, Smith's Luminary, Smith's Journal* and *Smith's Weekly Volume,* all general magazines. The magazine, *The Smith,* is a trade magazine for smiths.

IN MUSIC

Many famous pieces have been written concerning the smith, and world-renowned composers have used the Smith as inspiration. Perhaps the most famous are *The Harmonious Blacksmith* by Handel, the *Anvil Chorus* from the opera *Il Trovatore* by Verdi, and *The Blacksmith* by Mozart.

Other pieces include *Song of the Happy Blacksmith* by Bert R. Anthony, *The Blacksmith's Song* by G. N. Bordman, *Under the Spreading Chestnut Tree* by Charles W. Cadman, *Blacksmith* by Frank L. Eyer, *Jolly Blacksmith* by A. F. Harrison, *Forest Blacksmith* by Carl Heins, *Village Blacksmith* by Wallace A. Johnson, *At the Blacksmiths* by Carl Kling, *At the Village Blacksmiths* by H. Lange, *Village Blacksmith* by John Martin, *The Blacksmith in the Woods (Die Schmiede im Walde)* by Theodore Michaelis, *The Village Blacksmith* (Longfellow's poem set to music) by Charles T. Noyes, *In the Blacksmith's Shop* by Edmund Parlow, *Jolly Coppersmith (Der Kreuzfidele Kirferschmied)* by C. Peter, *At the Village Smiths* by Emil Sochting, *Blacksmith ana His Song,* by George Spencer. *Anvil* by J. M. Zimmerman. Two old glees are *The Smith,* by Conradin Kreutzer, and *Smiths are Good Fellows* by John Cobb, the latter having been written as early as 1667.

Many other pieces might be added to the above list as many composers of instructive music have written music to describe the smith and the smithy, especially since the advent of music for instruments with hammers. On the piano, especially, the music can suggest the rhythmic beating of the forge.

DENTISTS

Early dentists were smiths. Richard Locke Hapgood, in his *History of the Harvard Dental School,* discussing dentistry in colonial America, says, "The goldsmith, tinsmith, or blacksmith was the typical dentist in those days, and in most cases, his dental work was carried on simultaneously with and as a minor part of his usual vocation." Paul Revere was a dentist. On August 29, 1768, his advertisement appeared in the *Boston Gazette and County Journal,* as follows:

"Whereas many Persons are so unfortunate as to lose their Fore-teeth by Accident, and otherways, to their great Detriment, not only in Looks, by speaking both in Public and Private:—

"This is to inform all such, that they may have them replaced with false Ones, that looks as well as the Natural, and answer the End of Speaking to all Intents, by Paul Revere, Goldsmith, near the Head of Dr. Clarke's Wharf, Boston. All Persons who have had false Teeth fixt by Mr. John Baker, Surgeon-Dentist, and they have got loose (as they will in time) may have them fastened by the above, who learnt the Method of fixing them from Mr. Baker."

FAMILY MOTTO

Some families of Smiths use the motto:
"Smite quoth Smith."

"FABER MEAE FORTUNAE"

In his book *Life & Labour,* Dr. Samuel Smiles writes: "When a local historian of Somersetshire called upon Sydney Smith, while living at Combe Florey, to ask him for his coat-of-arms, the answer of the learned rector was: 'The Smiths never had any arms, but have invariably sealed their letters with their thumbs!'" The motto the witty divine afterwards adopted for his carriage was, *"Faber meae fortunae,"* which may be translated to "the Smith of my own fortune."

At the zenith of his success the late Lord Birkenhead (Frederick Edwin Smith) chose for the crest on his coat of arms the same motto.

A KING?

Anderson, in his book, *The Scottish Nation,* says, "In the Syriac, the word Hadad means Smith. There was a whole family of Assyrian kings of the name. Ben-Hadad means son of Smith, or Smithson." The kings were probably named after the Syrian god Hadad, well-known through the old Assyrian records, Aramaic inscriptions, etc. This word is similar to the Arabic word for "smith" which is *khaddad,* but Professor Robert H. Pfeiffer says that Semitic philologists do not seem to regard the two words as related.

SUPERSTITIONS

Smith-of-a-kind is a smith, the seventh in descent of a family of smiths. There is a curious superstition that when a child is ill, seven smiths, whose fathers, grandfathers and great-grandfathers have been smiths, collect in a circle, in the center of which the sick child is placed on an anvil. Those in the circle wave their hammers over the child's head, and utter with great force the stroke-groan *"Gegh."* If the child becomes terrified, the symptom is favorable; if it ignores their menacing attitude, all hope is forsaken. Each smith is paid sixpence, ale, bread and cheese. The charm can be worked with one smith only, if he is a *Smith-of-kind.*

Smiths will not light their fires on Good Friday. If necessity compels them to work in the shop, they will not start a fire, but will make the iron hot by striking it with their hammers until it becomes red hot.

SMYTHLAND

In 1616 there was an oxgang of land in Kirton-in-Lindsey, England, the tenant of which was bound to furnish the ironwork for four of the lord's ploughs. This was known as the Smythland. Elsewhere in England in feudal times some tenants could hold their lands only by working as a smith. When the lord required it, the smith might also be compelled to furnish him with iron. These lands were often called Smiths-land.

BLACKSMITH'S DAUGHTER

In some parts of rural England the house door key was called Blacksmith's daughter or Blacksmith's wife.

THE COOT

Smyth is a name given to the Coot *(Fulica atra)* in the Orkney Isles.

THE DAISY

In Scotland, a Scottish form of Smith, Gowan, is often popularly given to the daisy. The third verse of the ballad, *Annie Laurie*, begins,
> "Like dew, on th' gowan lying
> Is th' fa' o' her fairy feet."

COPPERSMITH AND IRONSMITH

A species of barbet *(megalaema faber)* ranging from India eastward to the Philippines is called by the natives by names meaning "ironsmith" and "coppersmith," because of its sharply accented metallic note. This bird is a gorgeously feathered sluggish fowl, making only short, heavy flights. Large numbers of them are found, quite noisy, but living only in the tops of trees.

ANOTHER BEETLE SMITH

A large scarabaeid beetle (*Cotalpa lanigera*) found in the eastern part of the United States, golden yellow in color, is called goldsmith beetle. The name is applied in a general way to all the beetles of the group *Rutelinae,* found in Central America.

SOME COMBINATIONS

1. Smith-body is a contemptuous term for blacksmiths.
2. Smith-corn was corn formerly given to smiths for sharpening the plough-irons.
3. Smith-ore is brown iron-ore.
4. Smith-wife, an obsolete term, denotes a female smith.

WHITESMITH

Whitesmith is a name given to a variety of gooseberry which has white fruit. The name is formed from the adjective *white* plus the surname of Sir William Sidney Smith.

GUNSMITH AND FINGERSMITH

A gunsmith is a slang term for thief. In thieves' jargon a finger-smith is a pickpocket.

THE RULE OF JOHN SMITH

This is the name popularly given that precept in the Bible, "For even when we were with you, this we commanded you, that if any would not work, neither should he eat" (II *Thess. iii,* 10). The colony at Jamestown at first operated on a common basis, the ignorant and lazy faring as well as the intelligent and industrious. It finally came to the point where about forty men were supporting the whole group. In the early spring of 1609 Captain John Smith called the colonists together and told them, quite plainly, that "he that will not work shall not eat," thus giving his name to the maxim.

SMITHIAN

This is a word formed from the surname Smith and has two principal meanings:
1. That which was devised or suggested by William Smith (1769-1839), the founder of stratigraphical geology.
2. Of, or pertaining to, the principles of Adam Smith.

ONE SMITH

"One Smith" may not be a very exact designation today, yet it occurs in Domesday Book under Essex—*"Unus Faber qui propter latrocinium interfectus fuit."*

ORPHAN ISLAND

Orphan Island by Rose Macaulay, a novel published in 1925, describes the life of three adults and forty orphans marooned on a desert island in the Pacific. When found, sixty-eight years later, the aristocratic, land-owning and ruling class was known as the Smiths, since they were descendants of Miss Smith, originally in charge of the orphans. The lower classes were composed of the orphans and their descendants who were not "Smith."

All actions were either "Smith" or "not Smith," meaning either upper or lower class, until the revolution when the Smith government and laws were overthrown and the name of the island was changed from Smith Island to Orphan Island.

SCHMITTSCHMITT

This curious double name is borne by two brothers in Chicago, who know of no others with the name in this country. Their grandfather, who came over from Germany about a hundred years ago, also bore the double name. Mr. William J. Schmittschmitt has made an extensive investigation of the family in Germany since the war, and has found, through the German post office only two of that surname in Germany. The name undoubtedly arose when two Schmitt families intermarried in a small village in Germany, and the double name was applied by townspeople as a sort of nickname, which in time became a permanent surname.

NICKNAMES

Of course, everyone named Smith is known as Smitty in America. In England inevitable nicknames for people surnamed Smith are Busky, Darky, Dusty, Ginger, Gunboat, Shoey, Smudger, Amouge and Tea Cake. These English nicknames arose mostly in this century in the army and navy.

GALLOWSMITH

Irvin S. Cobb wrote a story about a public hangman and titled it, *The Gallowsmith.*

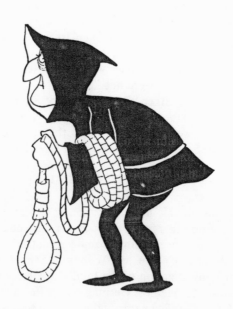

TRUESMITH

Woodrow Truesmith was a character played by Eddie Bracken in the movie, *Hail the Conquering Hero.*

THE DEVIL

In Aberdeenshire the devil is referred to as "Old Smith." This is from the black, dirty worker in iron, not from the surname.

ROKESMITH'S FORGE

Charles Dickens listed this in his notebook as a title for a book, but he never got around to writing it.

FRED SMITH

The Benevolent and Protective and Completely Universal Order of Fred Smiths was founded in 1936. They have held dinners in Chicago, New York, and elsewhere, attended only by Fred Smiths.

TNSDUNSPHI

The National Society to Discourage Use of the Name Smith for Purposes of Hypothetical Illustration was founded by Glenn E. Smith at the University of Minnesota when he grew tired of hearing a teacher use the name. Smiths all over the country have accepted membership. A member's solemn duty is to produce the membership card when he hears one with another name use the sacred syllable in an attempt to explain a mundane point.

GLENSMITH

In Scotland, John Robert White changed his name to John Robert Smith of *Glensmith* upon inheriting the lands of Glensmith.

IN JAPAN

There is no *th* sound in Japanese, and it is usually represented by *s* or *su*. Ruth is transliterated "Rutsu." When Art Smith, the aviator, was in Japan many years ago his name was written *Su-mi-su*. The Japanese commented on his unusual skill with an airplane because he could loop the loop not only in his plane but also in his name!

SMITH AT THE END

The termination *-smith* is frequently found as an egential suffix. There are Wordsmiths, Songsmiths, Rhymesmiths, Leathersmiths, Lawsmiths, Clocksmiths, even Colyumsmiths, among others.

CHAPTER 4

With The Jokesmiths

Hopeless
Breathless Visitor, "Doctor, can you help me? My name is Smith."
Doctor, "No, I'm sorry; I simply can't do anything for that."

It Hasn't Yet
Unmarried, "The worst thing about being a bachelor is that one's
     name dies with one."
Married, "What is your name?"
Unmarried, "Smith."

Two Classes of People in the World
1. Those who are named Smith.
2. Those who know people who are named Smith.

Always Give Your Real Name
Village Policeman: "What's your name?"
Speeder: "John Smith."
Village Policeman: "That won't do. We've had too many 'Smiths'
     about here. Give me your real name and be quick about it too."
Speeder: "Well, if I must, it's William Shakespeare."
Village Policeman: "That's better. You can't bluff a man like me
     with that 'Smith' stuff."

Take Your Choice
Ritz: "After God made all the people he named them, and upon
     finding a large, motley throng left over, he just named them all
     Smith."
Smith: "You have it wrong. At first there was just one tribe—the
     Smiths. When one sinned, the tribe forced him out and compel-
     led him to take another name. Now there are comparatively
     few of us left whose escutcheon is still unstained."

Smiths are Born, not Made
Sign over door, SMITH MANUFACTURING COMPANY.
Passerby, "Huh, so that's where all the Smiths come from."

The Sun Never Sets on the British Empire
Smith proudly, "The sun never sets on the Smiths."
Koliester: "No, the Lord is afraid to leave them in the dark."

What Lincoln Intended to Say
"God must like the Smiths, or he would not have made so many of
     them."

Memory
Smith: "My memory is so good that I can read ten consecutive pages
     of the Chicago telephone directory and then repeat every sur-
     name correctly."
Smythe: "I'll bet ten dollars you can't."
Smith: "It's a bet. I pick those ten pages devoted to the Smiths."

Spoiled Child of Fame
    A struggling author called on a publisher to inquire about a
manuscript he had submitted.
    "This is quite well written," reluctantly admitted the publisher,
"but my firm only publishes work by writers with well-known
names."
    "Splendid! That's great! Fine!" shouted the caller in great excite-
ment. "My name's Smith."

Mr. Smith

Under a flossy pen name a young writer named Smith had a best-seller published—a romantic book that was gobbled up by the public and the movies. On the strength of his success, the writer married, traveled widely, and was idolized by the ladies who sat on resort-hotel porches. Finally, all this adulation began to pall on the couple.

One evening they entered a swank hotel, and when the novelist picked up the pen to register, his bride said—in a voice that was overheard by the hotel clerk—"Why don't we just register under the name of Smith this time, darling?"

—The Wall Street Journal

Magic in Numbers

The story is that Pocahontas in pleading for the life of Captain John Smith used words to this effect: "Oh, father, please kill not this John Smith, for verily I hear that in the land of the white men there are many John Smiths, many times as many as there are braves in all the land of Powhatan; yea, as many as are the birds in the forests, or the fishes in the waters, so many are the John Smiths. Beware of provoking the vengeance of the John Smith tribe, else they will cross the big water in hordes and bring the thunder and the lightning in their ships. They will drench this land with the blood of our braves and their squaws. Oh father, spare this man and spare thy people." It is said that the old chief trembled at his daughter's words and granted her prayer.

He Got a Seat

Wag: (arriving late at crowded theatre), "Mr. Smith's house is on fire."

Such a great number arose that he was afraid he had caused a riot, so, acting quickly, he cried, "It is John Smith's house."

Two men sat down.

Probably

Headline in Newspaper—PARK STREET CLUB ELECTS J. D. THUMITH. Is this just a Smith with a lisp?

Homes for Them?
Police Sergeant, to the tenth person questioned upon being arrested
    in a raided night club, "What's your name?"
Answer, "John Smith "
Policeman, "I mean your real name?"
Answer, "John Smith."
Policeman, "Well, that's funny, you are the tenth John Smith in that
    place. What was it, a home for John Smiths?"

That most popular of poetry forms, the limerick, has occasionally honored that most popular of names, Smith. There
would certainly be more Smith-inspired limericks if the word
were more given to rhyming. Words that rhyme with Smith are
few indeed. Anyway, here are a few examples of Smith
limericks. By the way, the last example, which does not rhyme
correctly or make the slightest bit of sense, is included only
because its author was Mark Twain.

There was a young man named Smith
His name he was dissatisfied with.
        When called to the phone
        He would grumble and groan,
"I wish it was only a myth."

                                                    Clare I. Smith

Said a pretty young student named Smith
Whose virtue was largely a myth
        "Try hard as I can
        I can't find a man
Who it's fun to be virtuous with."

Miss Smith, who seems rather a prude,
And rarely appears in the nude
    Says the reason is simple
    Her prettiest dimple
Is placed where it cannot be viewed.

The marvels of nature I've never thought crude
Indeed, with its glories I'm deeply imbued.
    So I can't help but wonder
    What the dimple is under
If it cannot be viewed when she's nude.

A man hired by John Smith and Co.
Loudly declared that he'd tho.
    Man that he saw
    Dumping near his store
The drivers, therefore, didn't do.

                             Mark Twain

Seba Smith, whom we will meet later, was one of the earliest American humorists. His writings, usually in the form of letters, commented on the political and social scene of the early nineteenth century. He was considered particularly adept at catching the vernacular, back-woods speech of Americans. The example below is Letter XII from *My Thirty Years Out of the Senate*.

MR. DOWNING TELLS WHAT IT MEANS TO SET UP A CANDIDATE FOR OFFICE.

Portland, Tuesday, March 16, 1830
To Uncle Joshua Downing up in Downingville:
Dear Uncle Joshua:

There's a hot time ahead. I almost dread to think of it. I'm afraid there's going to be a worse scrabble next summer to see who shall go to the State husking than there was last. The Huntonites and Smithites are determined to have each of 'em a Governor agin next year. They've sot up their candidates on both sides; and who in all the world should you guess they are? The Huntonites have sot up Mr. Hunton, and the Smithites have sot up Mr. Smith. You understand what it means, I s'pose, to set up a candidate. It means the same as it does at a shooting match to setup a goose or a turkey to be fired at. The rule of the game is, that the Smithites are to fire at Mr. Hunton, and the Huntonites are to fire at Mr. Smith. They think it will take a pretty hard battle to get them both in. But both parties say they've got the constitution on their side, so I think likely they'll both beat.

They've been piling up a monstrous heap of ammunition this winter—enough to keep 'em firing all summer; and I guess it won't be long before you'll see the smoke rising all over the State, wherever there's a newspaper. I think these newspapers are dreadful smoky things; they are enough to blind anybody's eyes any time. I mean all except the Daily Courier, that I send my letters in; I never see much smoke in that. But take the rest of the papers that talk about politics, and patrotism, and Republikanism and Federalism, and Jacksonism, and Hartford Conventionism, and let anybody read in one of 'em half an hour, and his eyes will be so full of smoke he can't see better than an owl in the sunshine; he wouldn't be able to tell the difference between a corn-stalk and the biggest oak tree in our pasture.

Your neffu,

Jack Downing

Joe Smith and Charlie Dale, more popularly known as **Smith and Dale,** started their partnership at the turn of the century. Over the years they shared the bill with Weber and Fields, Al Jolson, Fanny Brice, Lillian Russell, George Jessel—everybody who was anybody in vaudeville. They performed their classic comedy sketch *Dr. Kronkhite* in theatres all over the country. Their humor was based on outrageous malapropisms and word play carried to the most manic heights.

Charlie Dale died in 1971. His partner for three quarters of a century, Joe Smith, now in his nineties and living in an actor's retirement home, had the headstone inscribed "Smith and Dale" and, he said, "when I go, I'll be next to him."

Below is a sample of the kind of fare that Smith and Dale delivered so brilliantly for so many years.

Smith and Dale's Ethiopian National Bank

DALE: (Enters) "Pardon me, is this the Ethiopian National Bank?"
SMITH: "Yes. I'm the president."
DALE: "Are you Ethiopian?"
SMITH: "If I were to do business under the name of the Eagle Pants Company, I don't have to be an eagle."
DALE: "Well, with your beak you could be."
SMITH: "Thanks—the feeling is optional. You came here for some purpose."

DALE: "Yes, I'm thinking of becoming a depositor."

SMITH: "Welcome. Now, how much do you want to deposit?"

DALE: "Don't rush me, first I want to examine you."

SMITH: "Examine me? I'm the president."

DALE: "I'm leary."

SMITH: "Mr. Leary, you're wasting my time. My time is money, and not my money either."

DALE: "I came here to deposit money and money talks."

SMITH: "Let's hear it."

DALE: "Good-bye" (about to leave).

SMITH: "Let's hear it."

SMITH: "Sit down—this is a friendly bank. Do you smoke?"

DALE: "No, but I chew."

SMITH: "Fine." (hands him an apple)

DALE: (About to take a bite)

SMITH: "Ten cents, please!"

DALE: "What are you doing? Selling apples?"

SMITH: "Just a sideline. Now. How much do you want to deposit?"

DALE: "First, where do you keep your money?"

SMITH: "I keep it in escrow."

DALE: "Escrow? Where's that?"

SMITH: "Some place near Boston. Now. How much to you want to deposit?"

DALE: "If I was to deposit my money right now—how do I get it out, by gas?"

SMITH: "You give twenty-four hours notice."

DALE: "I see you want to leave town."

SMITH: "Don't you trust me, haven't I got an honest face?"

DALE: "I'm not putting my money in your face. By the way, who's the treasurer?"

SMITH: "He went away for a rest, but he'll be out soon. Now how much to you want to deposit?"

DALE: "I want to deposit six dollars in quarters, a quarter at a time." (throws coins on desk)

SMITH: "This is a bank, not a slot machine."

DALE: "You don't get me."

SMITH: "I don't want you."

DALE: "I want to start a trust fund."

SMITH: "A trust fund with a quarter? Why don't you deposit a nickel and start a collection?"

DALE: "In case I need money during the night, what's your phone number?"

SMITH: "007-4321."

DALE: "Is that your home phone?"

SMITH: "No. That's a candy store downstairs, but they'll call me."

5

Smiths To Remember

OLIVER Wendell Holmes, in reference to a famous Smith, wrote: "Fate tried to conceal him by naming him Smith." But fate failed to conceal a great many men and women named Smith.

The Smiths of the world have attained their full share of lasting fame. *Who's Who* (1976-1977 edition) lists 217 Smiths and *Who's Who in America* (1976-1977 edition) lists 574 Smiths. In the immortal pages of the *Encyclopaedia Britannica, Micropaedia,* 53 Smiths are noted, which is more than any other surname. The *Dictionary of National Biography* honors 151 Smiths. The current one volume *Webster's Biographical Dictionary* lists 135 Smiths. The *New Columbia Encyclopedia* (4th edition) includes 46 Smiths; here John Smith and Joseph Smith tie for the longest space allotted to any one Smith. As Smiths lead in total numbers, so do they also lead in greatness. Smiths are not, as some people seem to believe, "born to blush unseen, unwept, unhonored and unsung."

Smiths have attained distinction in all lines of endeavor. Though they have always been pre-eminent in business and things practical, they can also hold their place in literature and the arts. Let us examine a single line thoroughly, one which is not concerned with the practical business of everyday life. As writers are found in all countries at all times, we shall take a look at that profession.

In Allibone's *Dictionary of English Literature,* 46,499 authors are listed, of which 810 are named Smith or 1.74 percent, a percentage far in excess of the proportion of the name to the population as a whole. Wilson is a poor second with 330 authors, then Williams with 325, Taylor 251, White 202, and Jones and Scott with 189 apiece. It might also be noted that of these 810 Smiths, 92 are named John, 79 William and 49 Thomas.

It would be impossible in a work of this kind to do justice to all the Smiths who have attained lasting fame. It would take not one chapter, not even one book, but several volumes to do the job properly. The purpose of this chapter, then, is simply to acquaint the reader with a few Smiths of accomplishment. All we can do here is touch on some of those Smiths who, through talent, intelligence, bravery or just circumstance have made their mark on the world. Some of these marks are black, because, though it pains us to admit it, not every single Smith has been a credit to his surname. If we have left out your favorite Smith we apologize, and offer as consolation the fact that if there were not so damn many interesting Smiths, we would have room for all of them!

In preparing this chapter, many sources were consulted. However, a special note of thanks must go to H. Allen Smith and his wonderful book *People Named Smith* (Doubleday, 1950).

Join us now and meet the Smiths!

ADAM SMITH

Of all good and great Smiths, none has had a more lasting effect on Western Civilization than **Adam Smith** (1723-1790). Born in Glasgow, Scotland and educated in the local schools, he later studied at Oxford. He was an industrious student and quickly rose to a level of prominence. In 1759 he published his *Theory of Moral Sentiments,* a dissertation on ethics, in which he embodied his fundamental doctrine that all moral sentiments arise from a feeling of sympathy. He was immediately recognized as one of the leading authors of the period. On March 9, 1776, Smith published his *Inquiry into the Nature and Causes of the Wealth of Nations* and soon became an authority on economics relied upon by statesmen and philosophers all over the world. Although written two hundred years ago, Smith's

ADAM
SMITH

work, generally known as *Wealth of Nations* is still useful today. It was because of this one book that political economy began to be regarded as a separate subject of scientific inquiry. Subsequent changes in the world that Smith could not foresee, such as the industrial revolution and changes in the nature and use of money, have diminished but not completely negated the contemporary relevance of Smith's ideas. For instance, his proposal for a division of labor in production processes was a forerunner of present day mass production. The word "Smithian" usually refers to the writings and ideas of this very great Smith.

SOLDIER SMITH

Smiths have always been ready to come to the aid of their country whenever necessary. As has been pointed out earlier in the book, it was the smith who was originally responsible for making the instruments of battle, such as the sword and armor. Smiths have proved time and again that they are just as adept at using weapons as they are at making them.

Sir William Sydney Smith was a British Admiral who made a name for himself defending Acre against Napoleon in 1799. He also fought at Toulon and was knighted for services to the King of Sweden during his war with Russia. A great showman and a compulsive quarreller, he was one of the most famous sailors of his day.

Lieutenant General Sir Arthur Francis Smith, of the famous Coldstream Guards, was one of Britain's great heroes during World War I.

Certainly the most famous Smith to fight in the Second World War was **General Walter Bedell Smith,** who served as Eisenhower's Chief of Staff. General Smith, known as "Beetle," had the job of coordinating the European invasion plans. As representative of the Supreme Allied Command, it was General "Beetle" Smith who signed the surrender papers. After the war, he continued to serve his country as American Ambassador to the Soviet Union.

Another great American Smith in World War II was **General Holland McTyeire Smith,** who served as commander of the United

States Marines in the Pacific. He too had a nickname—"Howlin' Mad" Smith.

In the War Between the States, two Smiths, one Union, the other Confederate, stand out.

Andrew Jackson Smith, despite his name, hailed from Pennsylvania. He was a brigadier general who fought through the Vicksburg campaigns and played a major role in the Union victory at Nashville.

On the Confederate side, the greatest rebel soldier named Smith was **General Edmund Kirby-Smith.** He was the last Confederate general to surrender to Union forces, which makes him a hero in many a Southern eye.

INVENTING SMITHS

The files at the Patent Office are filled with gadgets, useful and useless, thought up in the brain of somebody or other with the last name of Smith. If necessity is the mother of invention, Smith is at least a first cousin. H. Allen Smith dug through the files for a bit and came up with the fact that although no Smith has ever invented anything so important that it permanently altered the course of Western Civilization, there have been many important inventions hatched in the mind of Smith.

Charles Shaler Smith designed the first cantilever bridge in 1877. It was built for the Cincinnati Southern Railroad and crossed the Kentucky River. Two years later, Smith designed the first hanging railroad bridge near Canon City, Colorado.

Horace Smith and Daniel Baird Wesson collaborated on the invention of the Smith & Wesson revolver in 1857.

Hamilton E. Smith of Pittsburgh invented the first mechanical washing machine in 1858.

Hamilton Smith, no relation to the above, patented a tintype camera in 1856.

Sir Francis Pettit Smith took out a patent on a screw propeller in 1836, six weeks ahead of John Ericsson, the man usually credited with its invention.

The first pair of bloomers were stitched by a woman named **Elizabeth Smith.**

Major O. J. Smith invented the newspaper syndicate in 1882.

Joel West Smith of Connecticut invented the Braille typewriter after recasting the whole Braille system. He was himself blind.

Silas G. Smith invented the locomotive snowplow.

Angus Smith perfected a method of protecting iron pipes from corrosion by dipping the pipes while hot into a mixture of coal tar, pitch, resin and linseed oil.

Erasum P. Smith invented the word "telegram."

Lyman C. Smith, of *Smith-Corona* typewriter fame, invented the use of lower case type for use on typewriters. Before L. C. Smith's brainstorm, typewriters could only produce upper case type.

A few other smith inventions whose usefulness has not, to put it mildly, stood the test of time:

Elisha Smith—a gout nostrum.

Christopher H. Smith—"revolving glasses for spectacles."

Charles Smith—a hair restorer made from burdock root, Peruvian wood balsam, lemon juice, castor oil, slcohol, oil of roses, and rain water.

William G. Smith—a self-cleaning spittoon.

George P. Smith—walking stilts.

Frank E. Smith—an "office tickler."

William Smith—"a leg spreader for horses."

Ernest B. Smith—a trolley-wire cleaner.

Jay H. Smith—sticky flypaper.

Henry Smith—an undertaker's stool.

Oh well. They must have all seemed like good ideas at the time.

SOUTH AFRICAN SMITHS

In the nineteenth century, a great English soldier and adventurer named **Sir Henry George Wakeyn Smith** fought in South America, was with the British when they burned Washington, and was a brigade major at Waterloo. He also fought the Boers and Kaffirs in South Africa and after his fighting days were over was made governor of Cape Colony. He and his wife were so highly respected by the locals that they named two towns after them. Harrismith is the name of a town in the Orange Free State and Ladysmith was named after **Lady Juanita Smith.**

LONE STAR SMITHS

Smiths have figured prominently in the development of every state in the Union in one way or another. However, the Smiths of early Texas seem to have done a disproportionate amount of the work. Consider these facts: **Henry Smith** was the first and only provisional governor of Texas before its independence. Henry is also responsible for the creation of the Texas state seal. He just ripped the badge he was wearing off his coat, stuck it in some hot wax and *voila!*—the official state seal of the great State of Texas was born. Another great

Texan named Smith was **Ashbel Smith.** He was surgeon general of
the Army of the Republic of Texas, Texas Minister to England and
France and after that, Secretary of State. Which brings us to **Old
Deef Smith.** As his name implies, Old Deef was deaf, which wouldn't
be that unusual except that he was one of the most famous scouts in
early Texas history. Apparently, the lack of one faculty just in-
creased the capacity of the others. Lest people forget Old Deef, there
is Deaf Smith County on the panhandle plains bordering Mexico. By

the way, Texas also has towns called Smith, Smithfield, Smithland, Smith Oaks, Smith Point, Smiths Bluff, and Smithville.

EXPLORER SMITH

One of the most colorful Americans ever to bear the name Smith was **Jedediah Strong Smith.** It is odd that he is not as well known as Lewis and Clark or Daniel Boone or any number of other frontiersmen. His exploits were just as great as theirs, maybe greater. In an effort to right this wrong, his story is recounted here in some detail.

Born in New Hampshire in 1798, Smith received a fairly good education. At the age of thirteen he became a clerk on a Lake Erie freighter, learning business methods and, presumably, meeting traders returning from the Far West, all of whom had wild adventures to tell the impressionable young man. It is not known exactly when Smith first went west, but it is certain that he was with a fur trader named Ashley in 1823. Smith and three other men bought the business from Ashley, and spent the years between 1826 and 1830 exploring and trapping. It was during these four years that Smith made the journeys on which his fame as an explorer rests.

Leaving the Great Salt Lake in August, 1926, with seventeen men, he passed through the nations of the Utes, the Paiutes, and the Mohaves, and entered California from the Mohave desert in November, arriving at the Mission San Gabriel. This was the first time, as far as anyone knows, that California had ever been entered from the East and it marked an important milestone in the exploration of the continent.

Smith and his party wanted to continue north to Oregon, but the unfriendly governor of California, who was Mexican, would not permit it. However, Smith did proceed north into the San Joaquin Valley where he left most of his party while he and two companions attempted to cross the Sierra Nevada Mountains. After a false start or two they finally did cross the mountains and, more remarkably than that crossed the Great Salt Desert, another first. After a short rest, Smith began to retrace his route with a company of eighteen men. Unfortunately, the Mohave Indians were not as hospitable the second trip and they attacked the party and killed ten of the men. The remaining members continued on, made it to the San Gabriel Mission and proceeded back to the San Joaquin Valley where Smith had left the party the year before. Smith found the party in bad shape, but picked them up and started northward toward Oregon. They got as far as the mouth of the Klamath River when the group was attacked by the Umpqua Indians and everyone but Smith and two companions, who were away from the others, was killed. The remaining trio did manage to make it to Fort Vancouver and finally, without guide, got back to their original starting place, the Bear River.

Jed Smith had, understandably, had his fill of exploring and decided to retire, and went back to Missouri. His retirement was short lived because the next year, 1831, he joined on with a Santa Fe wagon train. That did not last long either. While out on a search for water, Jed Smith was surrounded by a group of hostile Commanches and killed. Although he was dead at the age of thirty two, Smith had already made his mark. He was the first explorer of the Great Basin, the first American to make his way into California from the East and out of it from the West. And he was one of the very greatest Americans ever to answer to the name of Smith.

SCULPTOR SMITH

One of the most influential American artists of this century was **David Smith.** It was Smith who revolutionized modern sculpture by using the remnants of industry for artistic purposes. Used tools, scrap metal and machine parts were his media and industrial welding his technique. By rejecting the traditional materials such as stone, wood and bronze and rummaging through junk heaps instead, Smith broke with the past and raised important questions about the relationship between art and life, as well as paving the way for generations of future sculptors. His work can be seen in art museums all over the world.

JOSEPH SMITH

One of the more controversial Smiths, and certainly the first one to come to mind when the talk turns to things religious, is **Joseph Smith.**

Born in 1805, Smith claimed to have had heavenly visions as a child. When he was eighteen, he said, an angel named Moroni appeared to him and told him of the existence of a book of gold plates containing "the fulness of the everlasting Gospel" and "an account of the former inhabitants of this continent." The location of this book was revealed to him four years later and, with the aid of magic stones called Urim and Thummim, he translated it into English from its original tongue, which was a form of Egyptian. Smith himself had little education and was barely literate. His translation of this revelation, called the Book of Mormon, was published in 1829 and won Smith many followers. He taught that his was the only true religion and that God had restored to him the ancient priesthood. Although his church held the Bible as sacred, Smith maintained that his writings and revelations were equally divine.

Because of the hostility of his neighbors, Smith was forced to move his church from New York to Ohio and from there to Missouri. Under Smith's leadership, the Mormons, as they were now called, lived in prosperous, self-sustained communities called Stakes of Zion. Unfortunately, the other settlers in Missouri were frightened of the Mormons and began attacking and persecuting them. Smith himself was arrested several times. Finally, he moved his church to Illinois and there established a monolithic church with its own militia. Through his claims of personal divinity, Smith ruled totally over all economic, social and theological aspects of the community. In 1884, he announced plans to seek the presidency of the United States. However, dissention over this and other matters was mounting within the Mormon community and Smith's opponents began publishing a newspaper called the *Expositor,* which attacked Smith bitterly. Smith destroyed the press to silence his critics and the neighboring non-Mormons, already shocked by rumors of Smith's polygamy, stepped up their harassment of him. Finally, he and his brother, Hyrum, were arrested and jailed. Three days later they were killed by an anti-Mormon mob. Later, Brigham Young moved the Mormons to Salt Lake City, their world wide headquarters today.

Today, the church that Joseph Smith began has over a million members.

CAPTAIN JOHN

One of the most romantic stories of the earliest days of America concerns the story of **Captain John Smith** and the Indian princess, Pocahontas. It is included in most history books on early settlers, and provides the basis for innumerable songs and poems. The trouble with the story, as with so much of John Smith's life, is that it is difficult to know for sure whether any of it really happened. We basically have to take Smith's word for it and his word, historians think, was not wholly trustworthy. He tended to exaggerate. Also lie.

Anyway, Smith was born in England in 1579. From his middle teens through his mid-twenties he fought in various armies for various countries against various enemies. According to Smith, he was captured and given as a present to the wife of a Turkish pasha. He eventually escaped and went back to England. In 1606, when the Virginia Company of London received its land patent, Smith claimed to have taken a great part in the formation and organization of the group. He sailed with the company for Virginia on December 19 and entered Chesapeake Bay the following April after a rough crossing, during which thirty-nine members of the party died.

Smith helped in the governing of the party, extensively explored the surrounding land, and dealt with the local Indian population to secure food. He was taken prisoner by the Indians, but was saved from execution by the intervention of Pocahontas, Chief Powhatan's daughter.

After he returned to the colonists, he was arrested and tried for the loss of two men in his scouting party and was sentenced to hang. He was saved by the intervention of Captain Newport, who had just arrived from England with supplies and food for the starving, quarrelling colonists. Smith continued to explore the Potomac and Rappahannock rivers as well as the Chesapeake Bay and in 1608 published a book on his findings. He governed the colony in 1608 and 1609, but was accidentally wounded and went back to England. He returned two more times on trading and exploring expeditions. His maps and experiences in the New World were the main source of knowledge for the Pilgrims. He died in 1631.

SURVEYOR SMITH

One of the great scientists was English geologist and founder of stratigraphical geology, **William Smith.** Born in 1769, Smith became a surveyor and soon became fascinated with geology. Through careful research, he discovered that the age of rocks could be determined by studying the fossils imbedded in them, thus laying the foundation for the science of paleontology. Smith continued his surveying work and later published the great geological maps of England on which his fame rests.

THE GIFT OF SMITH

Millions of Americans each year are the direct benefactors of a gift given by a Smith. **James Smithson** was the illegitimate son of Sir Hugh Smithson, one of the leading peers of England. James always resented the fact that he was deprived of an inheritance just because his parents were not married. Smithson grew up to become a highly respected scientist and, in his will, set up a fund of about a half a million dollars for the purpose of establishing the Smithsonian Institute in Washington "for the increase and diffusion of knowledge among men." John Quincy Adams, a congressman at the time, appointed himself as a kind of watchdog over the money and was largely responsible for seeing that the generosity of James Smithson was put to its intended use.

There is another reason for remembering James Smithson. The metal known as Smithsonite was named for him.

RASCAL SMITHS

As we said in the introduction to this chapter, not every Smith's contribution to the world has been admirable. If there is, as the saying goes, a rotten apple in every barrel, there are just too many Smiths around not to expect a few to be, if not rotten, a little over ripe.

George Joseph Smith, a rotten apple for sure, was an Englishman who lived in the early part of this century. It was Mr. Smith's practice to travel to a small village in England, meet a wealthy spinster or widow, woo and sometimes wed her and then quickly skip town with the poor lady's money. Twice he went so far as to drown his bride in her bath and tell the police she was subject to fits and seizures and must have had one while bathing. By constantly changing his name, and, of course, address, Mr. Smith was able to carry on like this for a number of years without detection. However, a London physician named Conan Doyle, who later created Sherlock Holmes, noticed the similarities between the cases and persuaded Scotland Yard to investigate. They did investigate, arrested Mr. Smith and eventually hanged him.

In American Revolutionary War days, a fellow named **Claudius Horseblock Smith** was the leader of an outlaw band and was known as the Cowboy of the Ramapos. Horseblock Smith ravaged the Hudson Valley, raising farms, harassing Washington's troops, murdering and stealing. He was eventually captured and executed.

Jefferson Randolph Smith got his nickname, Soapy Smith, because of a con game involving bars of soap and money, which he practiced on the streets of Denver in the 1880s. Eventually he was run out of town and moved his base of operation to the mining camps. He finally settled in a town called Skagway in the Yukon, opened a saloon, and, in general, took over the town's illegal operations, which were considerable. This being the Old West, the town's good guys finally banded together and put a bullet into Soapy Smith.

Jesse Smith was secretary to Harry Daugherty, Attorney General under the Harding administration. The team of Dougherty and Smith had been involved in bribery, swindling and shakedown operations in Ohio and after Harding was elected they just moved their base of operations to Washington. However, Smith began to crack under the pressure. He either committed suicide or was murdered, depending on who you believe.

Two Smiths were connected to Huey Long, the Louisiana demagogue. **Gerald L. K. Smith** was head of something called the Christian Nationalist Crusade, a racist organization similar in ideology to the Ku Klux Klan. **James Monroe Smith** was president of Louisiana State University. He was eventually sent to prison for manipulating that university's funds for his own purposes.

James Smith, a Democratic boss of New Jersey in 1910, got what was coming to him when he sponsored a Princeton professor named Woodrow Wilson for governor. Wilson won and, instead of playing the political game as expected, busted James Smith and his cronies right out of power.

C. Arnholt Smith was in the news during the Watergate affair. As a California businessman, Smith built a huge financial empire, which, upon investigation, turned out to have involved questionable business practices. He was also a good friend as well as one of the principal financial supporters of former President Richard Nixon. As of this writing, C. Arnholt Smith's business affairs are still being unraveled in the courts and the end is not in sight.

BUCKSMITHS

When it comes to making money, a little or a whole lot, Smiths show considerable talent. The number of Smith owned businesses would have to be enormous. Those inventors we met a few pages back certainly had money on their minds when they registered their ideas with the Patent Office. They weren't in it for their health.

Probably the most famous, or at least most visible, Smith ever to have a product bear his name is the **Smith Brothers** cough drop. The famous throat lozenges were originally made by hand by a Scottish carpenter named **James S. Smith.** When he died his sons, **William W.** and **Andrew,** took over. The little family business grew and grew and the company logo, featuring the bearded brothers with the words Trade (under William) and Mark (under Andrew) became one of the most famous ever devised. Today, folks with a tickle in their throat reach for the box with the brothers with the beard just as they have for decades.

Probably the greatest Canadian ever to have the name Smith, and one of the greatest Canadians period, was one **Donald Alexander Smith.** His energy and brains were the driving force behind the completion of the Canadian transcontinental railroad, a feat that had an immeasurable effect on Canada's development.

Cyrus R. Smith was for over twenty years president of American Airlines and his leadership is a major reason for that company's success.

A man named **Uncle Billy Smith** brought in the first oil well in Tutusville, Pennsylvania in 1859. Think what he started!

More recently, **Wilbur E. Smith** heads one of the leading urban and transportation design consulting firms in the world today, with thirty-five international offices.

And, of course, the number one brokerage house in the country today is Merrill Lynch, Pierce, Fenner and . . . that's right, **Smith!**

WRITING SMITHS

As was shown in the introduction to this chapter, the Smiths of the world do not seem to suffer from that old devil known as writer's block. A quick glance through the card catalogue of any library will produce many volumes, both fiction and non-fiction, from the pen of Smith. It would be impossible to list even a fraction of the Smiths who have been published. However, a few do stand out.

The man many people consider to be the first American humorist was **Seba Smith.** By writing in the back woods vernacular, he used humor to comment and poke fun at the American political scene of the time. His work *The Life and Writing of Major Jack Dowling* is a classic of early American writing. A sample of Seba Smith's writing can be found in Chapter 4.

Wintchell Smith was a highly successful playwright in the early part of this century. Among his successes were *Brewster's Millions, Lightnin',* and *The Fortune Hunter.*

Thorne Smith wrote a series of humorous novels about some very personable ghosts and their adventures which, collectively, are known as the *Topper* books. During the thirties and forties, his Topper books, as well as his other humorous volumes, enjoyed enormous popularity. The Topper books served as the basis for a movie as well as one of the early classic television series.

Betty Smith achieved fame as the author of *A Tree Grows in Brooklyn*, which, in addition to being a best selling novel was also made into a successful movie and turned into a Broadway musical comedy.

Lillian Smith made some big waves when she wrote a novel about an interracial love affair called *Strange Fruit*. It was a big seller in 1944, and is still selling well today.

More recently, a young man turned his career as a fire fighter into a best selling book called *Report From Fire Engine Company Number 82*. It was followed by two other volumes, *Final Fire* and *Firehouse*. Today, **Dennis Smith** is still writing and still fighting fires.

Mark Smith is a current favorite with fiction readers. His novels include *The Death of the Detective, Toyland,* and *The Middleman*.

SMITHS IN THE FUNNIES

Sydney Smith is well remembered by fans of the funnies as the creator of the "Gumps." In 1922 he received a million dollar contract from Captain Patterson of the *Chicago Daily News* ($100,000 a year for ten years). He died shortly after signing an even larger contract ($150,000 per year) in 1935, but his creation, the "Gumps" lived on with Gus Edson as his successor.

Al Smith played the successor role with "Mutt and Jeff," taking it over from Bud Fisher who had originated it and drawn it for twenty-five years. Al Smith has drawn it for the last forty-five years.

"Smitty" or as his younger brother Herby called him, "Thmitty," was a long running comic created by Walter Berndt. It featured the humorous adventures of a young office boy as well as his younger brother Herby, whose character later eclipsed his older brother's.

"Snuffy Smith" has had his billing raised and added to "Barney Google" is a currently running character in a comic strip now called "Barney Google and Snuffy Smith" as drawn by Fred Lasswell.

A LITTLE SMITH MUSIC

There is no way of knowing how many Smiths are, right this minute, taking piano lessons, singing in church choirs, strumming guitars before an open camp fire, playing the trombone in their high school band or in some way or other expressing themselves musically. However, it is fair to assume that the number of Smiths who create, teach and perform various forms of music is great indeed. A goodly number of Smiths have achieved lasting fame for their musical prowess.

The list of great jazz artists named Smith is nothing short of astounding. Greatest of all, of course, is **Bessie Smith,** the greatest blues singer of all time. Although she died in an automobile accident in 1937 at the age of forty-two, her records are still sold and enjoyed all over the world.

Another great blues singer was **Mamie Smith,** sometimes called the first true blues singer. Other great jazz singers are **Laura Smith, Clara Smith** and **Trixie Smith.**

A list of notable jazz musicians would have to include: **Ben Smith** (saxes/clarinet); **"Buster" Henry Smith** (alto sax/clarinet/guitar/arranger); **Floyd Smith** (guitar); **"Jabbo" Cladys Smith** (trumpet/trombone/vocals); **Joe Smith** (trumpet); **"Pine Top" Clarence Smith** (piano/vocals); **"Pope" Russell T. Smith** (trumpet); **Richard J. Smith** (trumpet/arranger); **"Stuff" Hezediah Leroy Gordon Smith** (violin/vocals); **"Tab" Talmadge Smith** (saxes); **"Tatti;; Carl Smith** (trumpet); **Warren Doyle Smith** (trombone); **"Willie" William McLeish Smith** (alto/baritone sax/clarinet/vocals); **"Willie The Lion" William Joseph Henry Bonaparte Bertholoff Smith** (piano/composer/vocals.)

The most popular Smith ever to break out in song was surely the great Kate—**Kate Smith.** A remarkably clear, to say nothing of loud, voice, coupled with her tireless efforts to raise money and morale during World War II brought her enormous popularity. Her rendition of *God Bless America* is the definitive one, and hearing it conjures up a whole batch of memories for Americans of several generations.

And that list, mind you, is of some of the greatest of *all* musicians. They just happen to have the same last name. There isn't a second fiddle in that whole list. Amazing!

Other musical Smiths who were not jazz oriented include **Ethel Smith,** a popular organist of the thirties and forties.

Francis Smith is remembered for having written the lyrics for one of the most often sung American songs, *America.* The tune for that is an old Prussian song.

Oliver Smith is one of the leading scenic designers for opera, as well as theatre, film and ballet.

Cal Smith, Carl Smith, Connie Smith and **Sammi Smith** are popular with fans of country music.

David Stanley Smith was a composer, conductor and, for forty-three years, member of the Yale University School of Music.

The music for *The Star Spangled Banner,* for which Francis Scott Key wrote the lyrics, is generally credited to **John Stafford Smith,** an English organist and composer.

Carol Smith, Donald Sydney Smith, Julian Smith, and **Malcolm Sommerville Smith** are all opera singers who have appeared in major companies all over the world.

SPORTING SMITHS

For some reason, the great name of Smith does not hold its own in the world of sports. One is hard pressed to think of any people named Smith who belong in any sports Hall of Fame. There is probably no reason for this, nothing in the genes that prevents Smiths from competing on the playing field. Nevertheless, it is true that though Smiths make the team often enough, they do not seem prone to greatness.

Probably the greatest Smith in sports isn't known by that name at all. Early in his career, Sugar Ray Robinson, the great boxer, changed his name from **Walker Smith.** True, he is known the world over as a Robinson, but that does not make him any less a true Smith.

Who can forget that tall Californian, cotton hat shading his face and blond mustache who captured Wimbleton in 1972, the top ranked tennis player, **Stan Smith?** Or the Dodger outfielder, **Reggie Smith,** whose resounding bat helped his team to the 1977 National League Pennant. Reggie was only the 12th player with the surname Smith to play in a World Series.

Otherwise the list is short. **Dr. James Naismith** invented the game of basketball, no small contribution to the world of sports. A horse named **George Smith** won the Kentucky Derby in 1946.

Speaking of horse racing, a young woman named **Robyn Smith** became the first female jockey ever to win a stakes race when she rode North Sea to victory in the Paumonik race in 1974.

Although Smiths do not fair too well on the field, they seem to have a great talent for writing about those who do. Quite a few Smiths are sports writers, the greatest of which is **Red Smith,** the Dean of American sports writers. He has been covering the sports world for so long and with such literate grace, that his name is often better known than the athletes he writes about. Red Smith won a Pulitzer Prize for Commentary in 1976.

ALMA MATER SMITH

Several Smiths have been prominent in the field of education. Having a college named after you, or naming one after yourself which is more usually the case, is just about the surest way to insure your own immortality.

Sophia Smith knew this when, in 1875, she founded Smith College for Women in Massachusetts. Today, its reputation for excellence is so high that it is one of the most prestigious colleges in the country. Of course, you don't have to be a Smith to get into Smith College, but upon graduation you will forever be a "Smithie."

One year before the founding of Smith College, another college, Wellesley, was founded. What has that got to do with Smith? Well, its founder was born **Henry Welles Smith** in New Hampshire, but was so unhappy about the commonness of his surname that he changed it to Durant. Smith/Durant was a lawyer and an evangelist before he founded his women's college. If he had named his college after his own real surname, Sophia would have had to come up with another name. Other Smith colleges are listed in Chapter 6.

SHOW BIZMITH

The mortality rate in show business is notoriously high. The number of folks with stars in their eyes is very large compared to the number who actually realize their dreams. If there is, as they say, a broken heart for every light on Broadway, then it's fair to assume that quite a few of those lights have the name Smith on them. A few

Smiths have, however, beaten the odds and lived to see their names above the title.

Gladys Smith made quite a name for herself. Who? Early in her career, Gladys changed her name to Mary Pickford and became known as "America's Sweetheart." The little girl with the golden curls was probably the first Superstar of the movies. Her marriage to Douglas Fairbanks made headlines, and their life together at Pickfair, their baronial home in Beverly Hills, was the subject of endless gossip. Gladys/Mary was also an extremely shrewd business woman. She turned the thousands she made from the movies into millions through a series of good investments. In 1976, Mary Pickford was awarded a special Academy Award for her services to the motion picture industry.

The beautiful **Alexis Smith** never changed her name and is glad of it. Her parents thought that Alexis was the feminine form of Alex. But having the most common last name and a man's first name didn't stop Alexis Smith from enjoying a long career in movies and theatre that is still going strong today.

The other great actress with the last name of Smith is **Maggie Smith.** In terms of sheer versatility and range, Maggie Smith simply has no peer in the theatre today. She plays the lightest of comedies one night and Desdemona in *Othello* the next. Maggie Smith won the Academy Award for Best Actress in 1969 for her performance in *The Prime of Miss Jean Brodie.*

Sir C. Aubrey Smith, whose movies frequently turn up on the late show, was another member of the tribe. Sir Smith was teddibly British, you know, and it was his Englishness which was his most distinctive quality.

Pete Smith was a producer of short subjects, known as Pete Smith's Specials, popular in the thirties and forties. His work was of such high quality that he was awarded two Academy Awards.

On television, we find **Buffalo Bob Smith** and his Howdy Doody Show. Millions of kids grew up on that classic children's program. In fact, twenty years later, Bob Smith has enjoyed a tremendous success touring college campuses with his freckled faced, red haired puppet and those over age kids are still crazy about him.

Other television Smiths include **Howard K. Smith,** the popular newscaster and anchorman on ABC, and **Jaclyn Smith,** one of the three women collectively known as *Charlie's Angels.*

Although she doesn't act or have a puppet show, **Liz Smith** writes about folks in show business with such good humor and style that she has become a celebrity herself. Her column in the New York *Daily News*, and syndicated in many other papers, is read and quoted by millions of people watchers.

VOTE FOR SMITH

Certainly the most famous American politician with the surname Smith was **Alfred Emanuel Smith,** better known as Al. Born in 1873 of poor Irish immigrants, young Al was forced to drop out of school at the age of twelve to help support his family. To escape the drudgery of his menial jobs, Smith became involved in the Democratic party. In 1903, he was elected to the state assembly, in 1913 became Speaker of the assembly and in 1918 was elected governor of the state, an office he held for four terms. Smith was a remarkable administrator. A forceful campaign style won him enormous popularity among voters. He threw out the old state organization, restructured the government, and put its finances on a sound bases. He also showed an interest in such problems as water power, social welfare, public education, and conservation.

Smith's success as governor encouraged him and his backers to try for the presidency. He tried for the nomination in 1924, failed, tried again in 1928 and this time succeeded. Unfortunately, he had too many things going against him in 1928. Herbert Hoover's great popularity, Smith's identification with the "big city," his "wet" stand on the prohibition issue and his own Roman Catholicism combined to defeat Smith's bid. He received only 87 of the 531 electoral votes. He tried again for the nomination in 1932, but was defeated by Roosevelt. Smith's active political career was over after the 1932 failure, but he continued to speak out on issues that concerned him, at the same time embarking on a number of business ventures, one of which was the construction and management of the Empire State Building. Roosevelt's New Deal alienated Smith from the Democratic party and in the 1936 and 1940 elections Smith supported the Republican candidates. Al Smith died in 1944.

The other great Smith in American politics is the lady from Maine, **Margaret Chase Smith.** Although only a Smith by marriage, she considers herself a Smith through and through. After completing her late husband's term in Congress, Mrs. Smith won election herself for three more terms. In 1948, against all odds, she won election to the Senate, making her the first woman in history to win a seat in that body on her own merits. She served in the Senate for a total of twenty four years. During those years, Mrs. Smith never hesitated to speak out on issues about which she felt strongly, regardless of whether or not she was following party line. Her speech against the infamous Senator Joseph McCarthy's witch hunt in the early 1950s became known as her "Declaration of Conscience" speech. She also took stands, long before such stands were commonplace, against the discrimination of women.

Ian Smith is the Prime Minister of Rhodesia. He is much in the news these days because of his country's continuing racial problems.

For other political Smiths who have made good—actually, made bad—please refer to the section of this chapter labeled *Rascals*.

FIRST LADIES

Although no Smith has ever made it to the Oval Office (Al came closest), there have been three Smith women who have held the title of First Lady.

Abigail Smith Adams has the distinction of not only being the wife of a president, but the mother of one as well. Her mother was a Quincy, one of the "best" families in Massachusetts, and her father was the Reverend William Smith. She married John Adams, a young lawyer, when she was twenty.

Abigail, by all accounts, was a tremendous asset to her husband. Their love letters to one another are still read today. They are among the most beautiful testaments of love and devotion every written. Besides advising her husband on political matters, Abigail took care of the family farm during the long stretches when her husband was away.

Probably the main thing Abigail Adams should be remembered for is that she founded the greatest dynasty in the history of the republic. Her son, John Quincy Adams, was elected President. Other direct descendants of Abigail Adams have held high government posts, serving their country as ministers and cabinet members.

Zachary Taylor's wife was the former **Margaret MacKall Smith** of Maryland. Taylor died after sixteen months in office, so his wife did not get much of a chance to prove herself. She was, however, a particularly colorful woman. She traveled with her husband during his war days, living with him in tents and stockades. And she smoked a corncob pipe, even in the White House. Their daughter, Sarah, was the first wife of Jefferson Davis, President of the Confederacy.

Bringing our account of First Lady Smiths right up to date, we come to **Rosalyn Smith Carter.** As this is being written, Mrs. Carter has lived in the White House only one year, but in that time she has endeared herself to the American public with her intelligence and Southern charm. Although a naturally shy woman, Mrs. Carter overcame her shyness to help her husband's remarkable campaign for the Presidency, shaking hands, giving speeches and answering questions with exceptional composure and knowledge. From all accounts, Mrs. Carter's advice is sought by her husband on a great many issues.

THE SMITH OF SMITHS

Though there are Smiths whose contributions to the world have been more significant and long-lasting, **Sydney Smith,** the great English author, humorist and clergyman, gave more people pleasure in his own time than anyone else. Lord Macaulay called him the Smith of Smiths, Charles Dickens named one of his children Sydney Smith Dickens, Queen Victoria was said to have laughed uproariously at his jokes and Abraham Lincoln read and quoted him constantly. Certainly, he is the premier jokesmith Smith of all time.

Actually, Sydney Smith was a preacher. Born in 1771, Sydney had a good education and was ordained as a minister in 1796. While working as a tutor in Edinburgh, he started, with a group of local intellects and wits, the famous *Edinburgh Review.* For a quarter of a century, Sydney anonymously used the *Review* to strike out against hypocrisy and tradition. He fought for parliamentary reform, among other things, but he is most remembered for his fight for emancipation of Catholics living in England. Eventually he became a canon of

St. Paul's in London. He probably would have risen higher in the church hierarchy, but his criticisms of the Church, as well as his devastating, merciless wit, prevented him. He died in 1845.

A few examples of his wit:

The people of Scotland, as well as their religion, were a constant source of inspiration to Smith. "It is in vain," Smith wrote, "that I

study the subject of the Scotch Church. I have heard it ten times over
from Murray, and twenty times from Jeffrey, and I have not the sm-
allest conception what it is about. I know it has something to do with
oatmeal, but beyond that I am in utter darkness." On another occasion, he said, "It requires a surgical operation to get a joke well into
a Scotch understanding."

He invented, during a sermon, the still popular expression for
describing a misfit—a square peg in a round hole. He once fed some
pigs fermented grain and reported that they were quite happy in their
sty, grunting the national anthem. During a hot spell, he exclaimed,
"It's so hot that I feel like taking off my skin and sitting around in
my bones." Another time he said, "The whole of my life has been
passed like a razor—in hot water or a scrape."

Criticizing the review of a friend, Smith wrote that he found it in
poor taste but "it is very able. It is long yet vigorous like the penis of
a jackass."

Smith hated country life, preferring the lights and saloons of
London, where he thrived. A lady once suggested, while visiting one
of the country places where he was compelled to live, that he ought
to have some deer on his estate. Smith stuck antlers on two of his
donkeys. The neighbors were shocked.

Smith had opinions on everything and he was never shy in voicing
them. He defended female education and scoffed at those who argued
that educated women would neglect their duties to the home, arguing
that it was most unlikely that any mother would "desert an infant for
a quadratic equation "

He was not above the occasional pun. His sense of humor was as
great when spontaneous as in the carefully written essay. One day,
while walking with a friend, he saw two women quarreling from opposite windows in a narrow street. "They will never agree," he exclaimed, "for they argue from different premises."

His humor was easily turned upon himself, especially in old age.
His aches, pains and infirmities just provided him with more source
material for his jokes. He was forced to go on a diet, which caused
him to complain to a friend, "Ah, Charles, I wish I were allowed
even the wing of a roasted butterfly." The resulting loss of weight
caused him to write to another friend, "If you hear of sixteen or eight-

een pounds of human flesh, they belong to me. I look as if a curate had been taken out of me."

When death finally came, Smith, true to the end, had a joke ready. He asked an attending nurse for his medicine, but the nurse found only a bottle of ink on the table where the medicine should have been. "You must have taken a dose of ink by mistake," she told him. Sydney Smith, the Smith of Smiths, replied, "Well, then, bring me all the blotting paper there is in the house."

CHAPTER 6

With The Versesmiths ›

SMITH

They haven't got a tartan,
 And they haven't got a clan;
Yet still they stand pre-eminent
 Of all the genus—man.
Unhaberdashed and unabashed,
 Unhyphened and unEed—
In all the history of the race
 The Smiths, they take the lead.

A Smith made bricks at Babel,
 A Smith flung stones at Troy,
A Smith—on good authority—
 Was Noah's cabin boy;
And when the Romans came to Rye,
 And lacked the landing pith,
The standard-bearer of the Tenth
 Was Quintus Marcus Smith.

In all the clever stories
  That men relate with glee,
Somewhere about the climax
  A Smith is bound to be.
In arithmetic problems, too,
  That vex the schoolboy brain
Smith is the man who walks so far,
  And goes so far by train.

And when the planets, swerving round,
  With wild chaotic crash
Collide, and grind together in
  The universal smash;
When this old world, in fragments flung,
  Shivers like splintered glass—
Unhaberdashed and unabashed,
  The last man—Smith—will pass.

                                        —*Anonymous*

SMITHS

We are glad to meet this happy day
  So many of our kin,
The grand old name would not betray
  The world's applause to win.

And proud we are to bear the name
  We speak it with delight,
And shall forever keep the same
  Inviolate and bright.

And now we'll trace our lineage back
  To Father Adam's birth,
And in fact, we shall nothing lack
  To prove 'tis old as earth.

The first, no doubt, was Adam Smith
    Who gave the world a start,
In the name was power and pith
    That won old Adam's heart.

And from the start in Adam's day
    The Smiths have held their own,
They came to multiply and stay,
    The fact is plainly shown.

Then we have the immortal John
    Of Pocahontas fame,
For whom the millions yet unborn
    Will gladly take his name.

No other name on earth so grand
    As thousands will attest,
The Smiths are found in every land
    The bravest and the best.

The name of Smith—a mighty name—
    A name to conjure with,
It brings to immortal fame
    'Tis surely not a myth.

Let those who bear some common name
    Make all the sport they can,
The first from whom creation came
    Were Smiths when time began.

But sad the fact, some soon went wrong
    And thought it best to change,
To other names both short and long
    From A to Z they range.

A few assumed the name of Brown,
  Others simply Johnson,
But poor the record these have shown
  We pity Jones and Thompson.

Then again some change to Smythe
  The Dutch all have it Schmidt,
But these have neither breadth nor height
  We cannot make them fit.

But listen, more amusing still
  The bloods will have Smithee
But none of them will fill the bill
  As we can plainly see.

These all have waged relentless war
  Contesting with their might,
But bless the Lord, we have no fear
  The Smiths have won the fight.

And when the years have passed away
  The whole of earth shall know
The Smiths with universal sway
  Shall rule the world below.

Now all the Smiths good courage take
  Be ready for the time,
A glorious record we shall make
  Immortal and sublime.

And some glad day when comes the time,
  We'll raise the Monolith,
And sweetest songs in cadence chime
  In eulogy of Smith.

So let the Smiths, their kin and kith
  A mighty host we know,
All all who boast the name of Smith
  The trumpet loudly blow.

And praise the Lord we've every kind
   Philosophers and sages,
Many of bright and cultured mind
   To bless the world for ages.

Then may the Smiths all be content
   No matter what shall come,
The name of Smith from Heaven was sent
   To bless the Christian home.

We pray their lives shall happy be
   All righteous, true and brave,
To reign and rule from sea to sea
   Our blessed land to save.

And may we all united stand
   With many years of grace,
For all that's truly great and grand
   The noblest of the race.

And if we shall united be
   In Christian purposes great,
Heaven's rich blessings we shall see
   In Nation and in State.

And when the grand assize shall come
   The renegades shall know,
Their certain and eternal doom
   To which no Smith shall go.

For those who cannot claim the name
   We'll take them on probation,
And when entitled to the same
   Will grant them full relation.

Hurrah for Smith with grand acclaim
   Let men and angels sing,
All praise and honor to the name
   In glory it shall ring.

With faith in God may all be blest
　　Trusting in His precious word,
And sweet in Him shall be our rest
　　In Christ our blessed Lord.

And now good-bye, 'tis kindly given
　　The Smiths to have this day,
May all at last meet up in Heaven
　　For this we húmbly pray.

　　　　　　　　　　　　　　—*C. D. Smith*

SMITH

Of all the ancient families that dwell upon the earth,
The most antique, if not unique,
Is that which gives us birth.
In every clime, from dawn of time,
Have dwelt our ancestors;
For on Egyptian obelisk,
And on the Grecian monolith,
You'll find enrolled in letters bold
The honoured name of Smith.
　　　　　—Contributor, Compton Reade's *The Smith Family.*

PREHISTORIC SMITH

Quaternary Epoch—Post-Pliocene Period

A man sat on a rock and sought
　　Refreshment from his thumb;
A dinotherium wandered by
　　And scared him some.

His name was Smith. The kind of rock
　　He sat upon was shale.

One feature quite distinguished him—
  He had a tail.

The danger past, he fell into
  A revery austere;
While with his tail he whisked a fly
  From off his ear.

"Mankind deteriorates," he said,
  "Grows weak and incomplete;
And each new generation seems
  Yet more effete.

"Nature abhors imperfect work,
  And on it lays her ban;
And all creation must despise
  A tailless man.

"But fashion's dictates rule supreme,
  Ignoring common sense;
And fashion says, to dock your tail
  Is just immense.

"And children now come in the world
   With half a tail or less;
Too stumpy to convey a thought,
   And meaningless.

"It kills expression. How can one
   Set forth, in words that drag,
The best emotions of the soul,
   Without a wag?"

Sadly he mused upon the world,
   Its follies and its woes;
Then wiped the moisture from his eyes,
   And blew his nose.

But clothed in ear-rings, Mrs. Smith
   Came wandering down the dale;
And, smiling, Mr. Smith arose,
   And wagged his tail.

                              —*David Law Proudfit*

AN ODE ON SMITHERY, 1610

By reading of old authors we do find
The smiths have been a trade time out of mind;
And it's believed they may be bold to say,
There's not the like to them now at this day.
For was it not for smiths what could we do,
We soon should loose our lives and money too;
The miser would be stript of all his store
And lose the golden god he doth adore:
No tradesman could be safe, or take his rest
But thieves and rogues would nightly him molest;
It's by our cunning art, and ancient skill,
That we are saved from those who would work ill.
The smith at night, and soon as he doth rise,
Doth always cleanse and wash his face and eyes;

Kindles his fire, and the bellows blows,
Tucks up his shirt sleeves, and to work he goes:
Then makes the hammer and the anvil ring,
And thus he lives as merry as a king.
A working smith all other trades excels,
In useful labour wheresoe'er he dwells;
Toss up your caps ye sons of Vulcan then,
For there are none of all the sons of men,
That can with the brave working smiths compare,
Their work is hard, and jolly lads they are.
What though a smith looks sometimes very black,
And sometimes gets but one shirt to his back
And that is out at elbows, and so thin
That you through twenty holes may see his skin;
Yet when he's drest and clean, you all will say,
That smiths are men not made of common clay.
They serve the living, and they serve the dead,
They serve the mitre, and the crowned head;
They all are men of honour and renown,
Honest, and just, and loyal to the crown.
The many worthy deeds that they have done,
Have spread their fame beyond the rising sun
So if we have offended rich or poor,
We will be good boys, and do so no more.

From William Hone's *The
Every-Day Book*, London, 1827

Following is a little known poem found in the British Museum Library. It was written about 1680 to commemorate a reunion of the Smiths in London and was published as a broadside by Francis Smith at the Elephant and Castle near the Royal Exchange in Cornhill, London. At the top in the center are two illustrations, one of two knights on horseback in full armor jousting; and the other below it showing a king presenting a banner to a knight in the presence of his men in battle array. Above these illustrations are two verses entitled, "Captaine JOHN SMITH sometime GOVERNOR of VIRGINIA."

Great Hero whose brave Sword in Martiaal field
Could Reap fresh Gorlies to Adorn his Shield
Whose Courage made y Turkish Cresents wane
Tnree of their Champions by him singly slaine

For such Exploits K. Sigismund (who knew
Honour a Tribute to his Valour due)
Three Pagans Heads in's Armes gave him to bear
Just Trophies of his Conquering sword and spear.

The poem in full follows:

A Congratulatory POEM upon the Noble FEAST Made by the Ancient and Renouned FAMILIES of the SMITHS.

      Ye happy *Muses,* who like *Banckers* fit
Distributing that precious Sterling, *Wit,*
Credit your Poet now with such a Store,
That his plum'd thoughts to that vast heighth may soar
Which all his Brethren ne're could reach before.
A more then common Stock ought to Proclaim
The Honours due to *Smith's* Immortal Name,
A Name whose early glories were so hurl'd
About ev'n in the Non-age of the World,

That other Families were hardly known
When this had waded far in bright Renown,
And by a Chain of Noble Actions bought
That envy'd Fame which others vainly sought.
Virtue and Valour, which at first alone
Could draw from dark Obscurity Renown,
In Ancient *Smiths* so pregnant did appear,
As if not Art but Nature plac'd it there;
As if she'd ta'ne a care to mould them so,
They must be famous if they would or no.

In *Germany* their Grandeur did appear
Long before *William, Britains* Conqueror,
And when that glorious *Norman's* Lucky Sword
Had giv'n him all our Nation could afford,
A noble Gratitude his Soul' did press
To thank one *Smith* for part of his Success,
Whom that great Duke was often heard to own
Mongst all his Captains, worthy great'st renown,
And in his private counsels held more dear
Than any other Martial Officer.

From thence if we proceed to that great Fight
Caus'd by the Invasion made in Eighty Eight,
Of none we read, excepting Mighty *Drake*,
Than Famous *Smith* that made more fierce attaque;
He made the haughty *Spaniards* feel his pow'r,
Giving them ruin on their Native Shore.

But why on Worthies past dost thou proceed?
Fond *Muse,* Thou liv'st too long amongst the dead,
Since, shouldst thou name the half, the sum would swell
My Pigmy sheet into a Chronicle;
And make the wondring stranger, when he came
To see so many Pages thatch'd with Fame,
Conclude, I write of Nations, not a Name:
'Twould be for thee more fit, for them more just,
To let them slumber in their Sacred Dust,

And (with a reverend leave) they Theam pursue
To give the Living, well as Dead, their due.

  Lift up thy long dejected head a while,
And thou shalt see within this narrow life
Thousands of their Successors who lay claim
To their Fore-fathers Virtues, well as Name:
Some thou wilt find whom their deserving Fate
Has justly rais'd to fit at Helm of State:
Others whose Loyalty did bright appear
At *Hogan's* Coast in the late *Holland* War:
Some there are likewise whose presaging worth,
Wanting occasion to be called forth,
Dos yet in silent Characters Proclaim
What Seas of bloud they'd make to wade for Fame,
Could they but face an Army which withstood
Their Monarchs welfare, or their Countries good;
And by Heroick Actions fain would tie
To their more Ancient, Modern Heraldry.

  For 'tis not the least Trumpet dos proclaim
Immortal honour to this deathless name,
That they like other lazie Families
Scorn on their Fathers Stocks alone to rise;
Each branch of *Smith's* great Stem looks sharp about
As soon as Sprung, to find new honours our,
Which like the Eagle viewing of his Prey
They fly full swoop at, and sweep clear away.

  Hundreds of ancient Arms at this day Crown
This mighty Name for acts of high Renown,
Which at the first from Foreign Toyls did rise,
Blazond with ruine of their enemies.

  But hold hot *Muse*, let's hear no more of War,
Since all the signs of joy and peace are here,
The sermons just now done, the Brethren wou'd
Not feast themselves, before they serv'd their God,

When Heaven with so much Plenty men do's bless,
They ought to have a Sermon for their grace.

   See how in friendly pairs the *Stewards Men*
To the grave Stewards give their due esteem:
See how the Stewards grandeurs do dispence,
Bearing white Rods, the signs of Innocence,
Which do not only their white thoughts imply,
But have respect to all the Company.

   Bless me! whose he comes here? A Mighty Lord;
Can he from all his pleasures time afford
To wast his minutes at a City Feast?
But he's a *Smith*, and so the wonder's ceas'd.

   See how in goodly order next do come
Whole ranks of *Knights*, the *Champions* of the Town,
Such heretofore in Romes warm Senate sate,
When *Carthaginians* thundred at her Gate.

A glittering train of Esquires next arise,
Like Sun-Beams, and set bounds unto my eyes,
Such who have often plow'd the Liquid Main,
And rang'd through Lands unknown for honest gain;
But these being past, the next my sight invades
Are worthy persons of Domestick Trades,
Hundreds of Wealthy Citizens, who buy
Their modest grandure with their Industry;
Men who in their narrow Shops can stand
And call for all the good things in the Land,
And have 'em brought them; they can Till and Sow,
And Reap, without the help of Land or Plow,
Receive their Quarter, nay their dayly Rents,
Although they own no Farms or Tenements,
And yet behold how glorious they appear
In modest Garments bringing up the Rear.

Having in short commented on them all
My Phancy too shall dine at *Drapers*-Hall,
Where it would feast a King methinks to see
Splendor it self begilt with Decencie.
Seav'n several sorts of Musick first advance,
And put my trembling *Muse* into a trance.
She well might fear that so much Art-full skill
Would drown the softer Cantos of my Quill:
But when she throws her lavish eye abroad,
And sees that plenty almost Cracks each Board,
Sees flaming Goblets by each Trencher set
As convoy unto every bit they eat,
Ready, if any dainty chance to stray,
To run down after and direct its way,
She recollects her self and fears no more
But sings much lowder than she did before.

Feast on, Renowned *Smiths,* methinks I spy
Contentment dancing in each members eye,
Nature and Appetite have now their due,
They are contented both, and so are you;
There's not a man but do's this truth assure
By his so free donation to the Poor.

The Widows thanks, and Orphans prayers discry
In quaintest Rhetorick your Charity,
Your needy name-sakes you do so prefer,
They become richer then their fathers were:
And when Maturity with age shall crown
Their greener heads, and they to Trades-men grown,
Why may not they gain Riches and Esteem,
And do for others as you did for them:
Thus by successive Charity you'll bless
Each other with a lasting happiness;
Ah! that this graceful Amity may prove
The little Embleme of Great *Englands* love.

And you, grave Stewards who this day fulfil
A Mighty Emperors Edict and Will,
Bearing in glittering Flags those Turkish-heads
Purchas'd by *Smith* of *Crudwells* famous deeds,
When 'twixt two Potent Armies he made fall
The strong Turbashaw, Turkys General,
And in the self same day, to crush the Pride
Of all his followers, vanquish'd two beside,
And brought their gasping heads besmear'd with gore
To·mighty *Sigismund* the Emperor,
Who thinking nought enough for that brave man
Who fought so stoutly for the Christian fame,
To make his royal gratitude appear,
Order'd three hundred Duckats ev'ry year
To be allow'd this noble Captain, and
Charg'd him by all the pow'r of his Command
Never again to enter Martial Field
Without three Turks-heads graven in his shield,
And sign'd a patten that the same should be
A Coat of Arms to his Posterity.

But I have been too tedious,—yet permit
Me to declare my wishes well as wit,
May evry action of each member here

To your successors bright as his appear,
May this great feast continue still, and may
Each year increase your Number, Wealth, and Joy,
Long may you live, and when insatiate Death
Shall call your bodies to perfume the Earth,
May your Examples your young Children move
To Rival you in Charity and Love.

JOHN SMITH

To-day I strayed in Charing Cross as wretched as could be
With thinking of my home and friends across the tumbling sea;
There was no water in my eyes, but my spirits were depressed
And my heart lay like a sodden, soggy doughnut in my breast.
This way and that streamed multitudes, that gayly passed me by—
Not one in all the crowd knew me and not a one knew I!
Oh, for a touch of home!" I sighed; "oh, for a friendly face!
Oh, for a hearty handclasp in this teeming desert place!"
And so, soliloquizing as a homesick creature will,
Incontinent, I wandered down the noisy, bustling hill
And drifted, automatic-like and vaguely, into Lowe's,
Where Fortune had in store a panacea for my woes.
The register was open, and there dawned upon my sight
A name that filled and thrilled me with a cyclone of delight—
The name that I shall venerate unto my dying day—
The proud, immortal signature: "John Smith, U.S.A."

Wildly I clutched the register and brooded on that name—
I know John Smith, yet could not well identify the same.
I knew him North, I knew him South, I knew him East and West—
I knew him all so well I knew not which I knew the best.
His eyes, I recollect, were gray, and black, and brown, and blue,
And, when he was not bald, his hair was of chameleon hue;
Lean, fat, tall, short, rich, poor, grave, gay, a blonde and a
        brunette—
Aha, amid this London fog, John Smith, I see you yet;
I see you yet, and yet the sight is all so blurred I seem

To see you in composite, or as in a waking dream.
Which are you, John? I'd like to know, that I might weave a rhyme
Appropriate to your character, your politics and clime;
So tell me, were you "raised" or "reared"—your pedigree confess
In some such treacherous ism as "I reckon" or "I guess";
Let fall your tell-tale dialect, that instantly I may
Identify my countryman, "John Smith, U.S.A."

It's like as not you are the John that lived a spell ago
Down East, where codfish, beans 'nd bona-fide school-marms grow;
Where the dear old homestead nestles like among the Hampshire
        hills
And where the robin hops about the cherry boughs and trills;
Where Hubbard squash 'nd huckleberries grow to powerful size,
And everything is orthodox from preachers down to pies;
Where the red-wing blackbirds swing 'nd call beside the pickril pond,
And the crows air cawin' in the pines uv the pasture lot beyond;
Where folks complain uv bein' poor, because their money's lent
Out West on farms 'nd railroads at the rate uv ten per cent;
Where we ust to spark the Baker girls a-comin' home from choir,
Or a-settin' namin' apples round the roarin' kitchen fire:
Where we had to go to meetin' at least three times a week,
And our mothers learnt us good religious Dr. Watts to speak,
And where our grandmas sleep their sleep—God rest their souls, I
        say!
And God bless yours, ef you're that John, "John Smith, U.S.A."

Or, mebbe, Colonel Smith, yo' are the gentleman I know
In the country whar the finest democrats 'nd horses grow;
Whar the ladies are all beautiful an'whar the crap of cawn
Is utilized for Bourbon and true dawters are bawn;
You've ren for jedge, and killed yore man, and bet on Proctor
        Knott—
Yore heart is full of chivalry, yore skin is full of shot;
And I disremember whar I've met with gentlemen so true
As yo' all in Kaintucky, whar blood an' grass are blue;
Whar a niggah with a ballot is the signal fo' a fight,
What a yaller dawg pursues the coon throughout the bammy night;
What blooms the furtive 'possum—pride an' glory of the South—

And Aunty makes a hoe-cake, sah, that melts within yo' mouth!
Whar, all night long, the mockin'-birds are warblin' in the trees
And black-eyed Susans nod and blink at every passing breeze,
Whar in a hallowed soil repose the ashes of our Clay—
Hyar's lookin' at yo', Colonel "John Smith, U.S.A."!

Or wuz you that John Smith I knew out yonder in the West—
That part of our republic I shall always love the best?
Wuz you him that went prospectin' in the spring of sixty-nine
In the Red Hoss mountain country for the Gosh-All-Hemlock Mine?
Oh, how I'd like to clasp your hand an' set down by your side
And talk about the good old days beyond the big divide;
Or the rackaboar, the snaix, the bear, the Rocky Mountain goat,
Of the conversazzhyony 'nd of Casey's tabble-dote,
And a word of them old pardners that stood by us long ago
(Three-Fingered Hoover, Sorry Tom and Parson Jim, you know)!
Old times, old friends, John Smith, would make our hearts beat high
        again,
And we'd see the snow-top mountain like we used to see 'em then;
The magpies would go flutterin' like strange sperrits to 'nd fro,
And we'd hear the pines a-singing' in the ragged gulch below;
And the mountain brook would loiter like upon its windin' way,
Ez if it waited for a child to jine it in its play.

You see, John Smith, just which you are I cannot well recall,
And, really, I am pleased to think you somehow must be all!
For when a man sojourns abroad awhile (as I have done)
He likes to think of all the folks he left at home as one—
And so they are! For well you know there's nothing in a name—
Our Browns, our Joneses and our Smiths are happily the same;
All represent the spirit of the land across the sea,
All stand for one high purpose in our country of the free!
Whether John Smith be from the South, the North, the West, the
        East—
So long as he's American, it mattereth not the least;
Whether his crest be badger, bear, palmetto, sword or pine,
He is the glory of the stars that with the stripes combine!
Where'er he be, whate'er his lot, he's eager to be known,
Not by his mortal name, but by his country's name alone!

And so, compatriot, I am proud you wrote your name today
Upon the register at Lowe's, "John Smith, U.S.A."

—*Eugene Field*

Taken by permission from Eugene Field:
John Smith U.S.A., published and copyright by
Mr. A. Donohue & Company, Chicago.

THE CLAN SMITH

From Scotland and from Ireland to our golden shore
America is mighty proud of her adopted sons galore,
There is the clan O'Shaughnessy, also the clan of Moore,
Who love the land of sunshine, but love the old sod more;
There are the Tooles, the Hannigans, and the Bradys, too,
And of the clan O'Hara there is quite a few,
And not a single family we are acquainted with
Can compare a minute with the good old clan of Smith!

They do be saying there are those who want to make a change,
And to one who ever knew them this sounds a wee bit strange,—
For the name that one is born with is an early heritage
And often it's the only thing that's left in one's old age;
The Irish and the Scotch are known in family clan,
And the name that they are known by is the pride of every man;

But the finest clan among us which we are acquainted with
Is the clan that's known to every one as the clan of Smith!

They do be telling of a tale reaching back a million years—
The world was in its infancy, the people had no cares;
They do be after saying that then the name of Smith
Was the only one that any one was then acquainted with;
The judge of the recorder's court was jealous of the name,
As the judge's patronymic also was the honored same,
And every single culprit who before the old judge came
Was sentenced, besides dire punishment, forthwith to change his
      name!

                              —Earle E. Griggs

SMITH-DAY

They extend an invitation to each Smith upon the earth—
Old an' young an' short an' tall Smiths, Smiths of high an' humble
      birth;
Smiths of wealth, an' poor an' far Smiths, homely Smiths, an'
      others, too;
To unite with them enjoyin' such another Smith "to-do!"
Smiths of Smithville, Smiths of Smithers, Smiths of Smitters, will
      be there.
An' they'll have the fines' frolic that has happened anywhere.
Smiths from Georgia, Smiths from Texas, Smiths from every
      Southern State,
Will for this auspicious 'casion to old Macon emigrate!

If a member of this family, make your plans now for the trip;
You could not afford to miss it—seems to me I'd fuss and rip
Were I one among the number an' could not the funnin' share
That is gwine to be presented on this Smith Day at the Fair.

                              —Ernest Camp

SMITH-DAY

It's "Howdy Smith," and "Hello Smith," and "Smith, old boy,"
      today,
And "Come on, Smith, it's one on me—the Smiths don't have to
      pay;"

It's "How is Mrs. Smith?" and "How's the little Smiths a-doin'?"
And every blessed Smith is here from Rabun Gap to ruin.

It's Major Smith, and Colonel Smith, and Captain Smith, and there
Are two Smiths that are candidates to be here at the fair,
And Reverend Smith, and 'Fessor Smith, and Doctor Smith; the
        sight'll
Be worth the seeing, and there'll be the Smith without a title.

There's handsome Smiths and homely Smiths and av'rage Smiths
        between,
Just any sort o' Smith you like can easily be seen;
And Smiths of every calling and profession you can muster,
With all the Christian and un-Christian names from Bill to Buster.

Here's to the whole big, jolly tribe of Smiths of every kind—
A brighter, better, bigger-hearted lot you'll never find;
Be glad there's not a fam'ly in this Anglo-Saxon nation
That hasn't somewhere, somehow, got a Smith for a relation.
                              —From *The Macon Telegraph*
                                reprinted in *The Atlanta*
                            Constitution of October 29, 1905

JOHN SMITH

A mighty crowd had assembled that night
To watch the battle in a big prize fight.
The umpire rose and said that a wire
Announced that Mr. Smith's house was a-fire.
A number of men, a thousand and four,
Arose with a rush and made for the door.

The announcer then said *John* Smith was the name
Of the man whose house they said was a-flame.
One frail little man, who was dressed very neat,
Was seen sinking back, resuming his seat;
"Thank God," those near him heard him say,
While the rest of the Smiths all scurried away.
                                          —*J. M. Quindry*

THE LAMENT OF A SMITH

O that my name were Brown, or Bright,
Or Evans, Thomas, Jones, or White;
Or anything else—it makes no diff.—
Except this miserable name of Smith!

Full seven-and-twenty in college here
Keep me in confusion all the year;
And woe is me!—whate'er my gift—
I'm ne'er distinct from the tribe of Smith.

My efforts fail—my work's in vain
Because of my confounded name;
I'd have been famous long since if
My name were anything else but Smith.

Disgusting! To possess this name,
And, howe'er well deserving fame,
Be talked of, thought of, catalogued with
The common crowd by the name of Smith!

O that my name were Brown, or Bright,
Or anything else—it makes no diff.—
O that my name were Jones, or White,
Or anything but this name of Smith!

—1896 *Badger,* Yearbook of
University of Wisconsin

THE SMITH'S SONG

Ring, ring, ringing! Iron with iron is singing!
'Tis pleasant to me, as the sound of the sea,
When the spring morning tide, comes as to bride,
Kissing the shore, with a rippling greeting.

Sing, sing, singing! still on the air comes winging
The very refrain, heard by old Tubal Cain,
When, from prison of stone, came the metal alone,
And Iron, with iron, seemed to carol at meeting.

The smith, they say, he works all day, hard labour and much din,
You rarely see him ever free, from smoky, toil-stain'd skin;
But work-stained face, bars not God's grace—our ancient, useful art
Makes skin be tann'd, gives horny hand, but never hardened heart.

And yet its rough, and black, and tough, that metal that you mould,
It has no light, of the silver bright, nor gleam of the lordly gold.
But from it is made, the pick and spade, that win them both from
    earth,
And the weapon keen, has power, I ween, to keep the home and
    hearth;

And the needle that guides, and the ship that glides, o'er the waves
    where the winds but tread,
And the needle that flies, after eager eyes, in the race for beauty or
    bread;
The smith brings aid, to every trade, and has done since the world
    was young—
"By hammer and hand all arts do stand!" may still, as of yore, be
    sung.

Ring, ring, ringing! still to the ear come winging,
The notes true and clear, they are cheering to hear,
'Tis Nature herself who a carol is singing!

                       —*Edward Quaile*

THE SMITH AND THE KING

A Smith upon a summer's day
    Did call upon a king.
The king exclaimed: "The queen's away;
    Can I do anything?"

"I pray you can," the smith replied;
    "I want a bit of bread."
"Why?" cried the king. The fellow sighed;
    "I'm hungry, sire," he said.

"Dear me! I'll call my chancellor;
    He understands such things.
Your claims I cannot cancel or
    Deem them fit themes for kings.

"Sir chancellor, why here's a wretch,
    Starving—like rats or mice!"
The chancellor replied: "I'll fetch
    The first lord in a trice."

The first lord came, and by his look
    You might have guessed he'd shirk.
Said he: "Your Majesty's mistook;
    This is the chief clerk's work."

The chief clerk said the case was bad
    But quite beyond his power,
Seeing it was the steward had
    The keys of cake and flour.

The steward sobbed: "The keys I've lost!
  Alas! but in a span
I'll call the smith. Why heavens above!
  Here is the very man!"

"Hurrah! hurrah!" they loudly cried;
  "How cleverly we've done it!
We've solved this question deep and wide,
  Well-nigh ere we begun it."

"Thanks," said the smith. "O fools and vile,
  Go rot upon the shelf!
The next time I am starving I'll
  Take care to help myself."

—Edward Carpenter

"A habit rather blamable, which is
  That of despising those we combat with,
Common in many cases, was in this
  The cause of killing Tchitchitzkoff and Smith;
One of the valorous 'Smiths' whom we shall miss
  Out of those nineteen who late rhymed to 'pith';
But a name so spread o'er 'Sir' and 'Madam,'
  That one would think the first who bore it 'Adam'".

From Lord George Gordon Byron:
Don Juan, Stanzas xviii and xxv,
Canto VII.

"Before she visited his ship she wanted him to say
If the Smythes had recognized him in a social, friendly way:

Did the Jonsons ever ask him 'round to their ancestral halls?
Was he noticed by the Thomsons? Was he asked to Simms's balls?

The pirate wrote that Thomson was his best and oldest friend,
That he often stopped at Jonson's when he had a week to spend;
As for the Smythes, they worried him with their incessant calls;
His very legs were weary with the dance at Simms's balls.

(The scoundrel fibbed most shamelessly. In truth he only knew
A lot of Smiths without a y—a most plebeian crew.
His Johnsons used a vulgar h, his Thompsons spelled with p,
His Simses had one m, and they were common as could be.)"
                              —From Max Adeler: *Out of the Hurly-*
                                       Burly—"Mrs. Jones's Pirate"

"Smiths! the Smiths are hydra-headed;
   Smiths grow up three deep in rows;
Smiths in countless hosts and legions,
   Everywhere have poked their nose."

                                              —*A. Wingfield*

"High on the roll of men renowned,
Who had their birth on English ground,
The name of Smith shall ever stand,
An honour to his native land."

                              —From J. H. Martin: *Smith*
                                        and Pocahontas

MODERN VERSON
Beneath the spreading chestnut tree,
   The horses' tails are swishin',
The smith, a prideful man is he—
   He's known as a horsetician!

                                              —Anonymous

CHAPTER 7

On Smith

THE most famous quotation concerning names is from Shakespeare's *Romeo and Juliet* where Juliet exclaims,
"What's in a name? that which we call a rose
By any other name would smell as sweet."
Carlyle said, "There is much, nay, almost all in names. The name is the earliest garment wrapt around the earth, to which it thenceforth cleaves more tenaciously than the very skin. There are names which have lasted nigh thirty centuries. Not only all common speech, but science—poetry itself—is no other, if thou consider it, than a right naming."
Many things have been said and written about the name of Smith. A few will be quoted. Betsey Trotwood (in *Home Journal*) wrote: "The name of Smith could, certainly, never be made to sound either beautiful or patrician, and any attempt either way would produce only a ludicrous effect. That it can be somewhat modified, no one will doubt who can appreciate the advantage Sidney Smith possessed over Alexander Smith. There is one redeeming trait in Smith—the very want of distinctiveness in the name seems that it shall always be used with the Christian-name affixed. The best that can be done for Smith is to raise it from commonness to mere ugliness. Some curious name joined to Smith would take attention from it."

In contrast with that disgruntled outburst the following extract was written by philosopher and writer, Gilbert K. Chesterton from his *Heretics:* "In the case of Smith, the name is so poetical that it must be an arduous and heroic matter for the man to live up to it.... Yet our novelists call their hero 'Aylmer Valence', which means nothing, or 'Vernon Raymond', which means nothing, when it is in their power to give him this sacred name of Smith—this name made of iron and flame. It would be very natural if a certain hauteur, a certain carriage of the head, a certain curl of the lip, distinguished every one whose name is Smith. Perhaps it does; I trust so. Whoever else are parvenus, the Smiths are not parvenus. From the darkest dawn of history this clan has gone forth to battle; its trophies are on every hand; its name is everywhere; it is older than the nations, and its sign is the hammer of Thor.....If you think the name of 'Smith' prosaic, it is not because you are practical and sensible; it is because you are too much affected with literary refinements. The name shouts poetry at you. If you think of it otherwise, it is because you are steeped and sodden with verbal reminiscences, because you remember everything in *Punch* or *Comic Cuts* about Mr. Smith being drunk or Mr. Smith being henpecked. All these things were given to you poetical. It is only by a long and elaborate process of literary effort that you have made them prosaic."

An anonymous writer (in *Chambers's Edinburgh Journal)* under the title, *Smith, You Know!* wrote: "In the passages of life, if there be a theme truly grateful to the heart and absorbing to the mind, which sovereignly interests, nay takes the whole soul captive; if there by any one topic calculated to awaken to a sense of the positive, and snatch us from the misty regions of romance, which, compelling, us from the contemplation of the vague, the visionary, the ideal, forces us face to face, heart to heart, with the things of earth, and hurries us into the very council-chamber and stately presence of the real; if there be a subject omnipotent in expression, powerful in mystic meaning, wide-spread in its influences, unchangeable in its essence, and marvelous in its destiny, assuredly that theme, that subject, that all-absorbing topic is comprised in that wondrous impersonation—*Smith!"*

*   *   *   *   *

"What heart does not throb with delicate sentiments; whose pulse does not beat with pleasurable emotion; what cheek is not suffused with joy; whose blood does not run more genially; whose spirit is not moved to the very depths, whenever the mystic monosyllable is pronounced!"

* * * * *

"Smith is an evergreen, a perennial, a flower always in bloom, replete with beauty and vigour, ever new, a true *'immortelle'*, which decay can never touch; the delight of every eye, the charm of every heart, a hymn of welcome, a magic spell, a talisman, a theme for poets, historians, philosophers, in itself a sublime epic."

* * * * *

An editorial writer in the *Atlanta Constitution* of March 19, 1905, wrote: "The man who carries the melodious cognomen of Smith may flatter himself that his ancestors bore an excellent reputation in the society of their time. They were not drones or laggards. They were workers, they 'MADE' something."

* * * * *

"They did not bequeath to their descendants the many-syllabled, mellow-toned names, which many of our modern families bear, but they did hand down a legacy of industry and enterprise, and even in rogues we are bound to admire these qualities. In spite of the obloquy which some people reflect on this sturdy ancestry by inserting a hyphen between Smith and some other distinguishing pendent, the enormous family is still multiplying and thriving and DOING THINGS as fervently and unremittingly and intelligently in the very present future as throughout the vague and crowded past. Indeed from the standpoint of multiplication, every country under the sun owes a notable debt to the tribe of Smith.

"Let not the future historian of the ilk of Smith overlook these vital facts. When that mooted, mythical monument shall be erected with the joint contributions of the world's united Smiths, let the sculptor carve on the pedestal, in bold, belligerent letters— 'MAKERS OF SOMETHING.' "

SOCIAL REGISTER SMITHS

The proverb, "Smith, Jones, Brown and Robinson", is often used to designate the *ignoble vulgus,* and perhaps for this reason many Smiths are ashamed of their name and often try to hide it. This attitude is ridiculous, but it does exist, especially in England where birthright is regarded with much more esteem than in this country. The true fact is that in this country the Smiths are among the elite. For proof we need only look at the New York Social Register. In the many editions one finds that the Smiths far outnumber any other name. The Browns are usually second with the Williams third and the Clarks fourth. Then come the Millers, Joneses, Walkers and Johnsons, in that order. The Smiths, in proportion to other names, often rank higher in the Register than they do in the city directory.

The English genealogist, Reade, in collecting material for his genealogy of the Smith family, found that many Smiths refused to give him their pedigree because of pride, and observed, "Whereupon I have to remark, that if, as I have found, Messieurs les Smiths choose to regard their name and parentage as a byword and reproach, they need scarcely feel surprised if the world takes them at their own valuation."

He tells the following: "A mansion with ancient rookery was purchased by a man supposed to be named Smith, and the rooks, whose tenure of the Elizabethan elms was as ancient as the mansion, met in conclave and decided that if would be beneath their dignity to adorn the demesne of anyone with so plebeian a patronymic. They were in fact about to migrate, when one of their tribe arrived post haste to assure them that the name was Smythe and not Smith. That of course altered the case, and they unanimously decided to remain."

There are still a few social-climbers and others anxious to keep what little finger-hold they may have on the social ladder who go on the assumption that "family" is everything and whose attitude is, to quote the words of Max Adeler's Mrs. Jones, "The Smith that spells without a y is not the Smith for me!"

Those who say that Smith is a base name and plebeian in origin might look at some of the distinguished and honorable names which are derived from *swine:* Bacon, Everett, Everts, Hogarth, Hogg, Pigg, Stewart, Sugden, Swain, Swinburne, Swinton.

H. C. Lawlor, in an article in the *Proceedings and Reports of the Belfast Natural History and Philosophical Society,* quotes a writer from a monograph entitled, *How to Compile a Pedigree,* after suggesting that one need not be hoi poloi when it is so easy to acquire a respectable pedigree, as follows:

THE CARRINGTON CASE

"Unquestioned evidence proves beyond doubt the following facts:—In the years 1442 and 1466 a farm known as Archer's in the Parish of Rivenhall, Essex, was in occupation of one Thomas Smith, yeoman. Another Thomas, evidently son of the first, was in possession in 1498. The next recorded as in possession was Sir Clement Smith, Knight who died in 1551. Sir Clement was the first of the family to obtain a prominent position, and died possessed not only of the farm where he was born, but other lands. From his time an ex-

traordinary run of marriages with heiresses raised the family in a few
generations to one of influence and wealth. A brother, apparently of
the first mentioned Thomas Smith, by name Hugh Smith of
Witham, had a son John who was a lawyer. He prospered and was
made a Knight and obtained from the Garter King, Edward III of
England, a brand new coat of arms. He married the heiress of a good
estate in Warwickshire, and the son of the marriage inherited the es-
tates of both parents and himself married the heiress of Ashby
Folville in Lincolnshire.

"This carries the family on to about 1585, when the Smith of the
day, Henry by name, owner of broad lands and wealth, with wealthy
and influential connections and lofty ambitions, found himself with
his plebeian name of Smith, looked upon by those of whom he
longed to be one, as a mere upstart. His grief was real. How could a
common Smith become noble and sit on those exalted benches of the
house of Lords beside all those heirs of Norman and Saxon Barons
like the Berties, or the Geraldines whose pedigree began with the
siege of Troy? The old problem of making a silk purse out of a sow's
lug daily and nightly stared him in the face and wore him to a
shadow. Who could solve such a problem? Well Henry Smith did.
He opportunely produced an ancient parchment which he had discovered in an ancient chest in a long disused chamber in his ancestral
home. This parchment purported to be 'Ye confession of me, John
Smith or Carrington.' It was a simple tale of a simple man, evidently
for very simple people, purporting to have been written on his
deathbed about the year 1440, in the beautiful English in vogue
about the year 1600. It contained a heartrending story of the writer,
who had been a lifelong and ardent supporter of Richard II. When
that unfortunate Monarch fell under the power of the usurper Henry
IV, this loyal adherent, out of protest, left the country and lived in
Gascony. In 1404 he felt a longing to revisit his native land, and
returned, landing at Ipswich 'whence on ye morrow he rid to St.
Nees, disclosing himself to his cousin there, ye Abbot, his father
Carrington's sister's son by Sir John Curzon'. The Abbot,
astonished to see him, warned him of the cruelty of Henry IV to all
the adherents of Richard II and advised him to dissemble. Hence he
pretended to be one, John Smith, which pretence he had closely
adhered to, hiding the fact that he was really the second son of Sir

Thomas Carrington who descended from that Sir Michael Carrington standard bearer to Richard I in his crusades (a perfectly mythical person, by the way). The old manuscript was full of careful detail, a little too full in places unfortunately, but it proved a godsend to the lucky Smith, who found himself suddenly raised from being a common or garden Smith to the rank and position of a real Norman Carrington with a pedigree extending unbroken from the Conquest. What more could he want? He was soon created Earl of Carrington, and his noble descent duly enrolled in the office of arms on the payment of the proper fees. I have no doubt it took a decent fee to get it all swallowed, but it was. In due time in Ashby Folville Church were laid to rest, beside the remains of the lawyer, Sir John Smith, those of the noble Earls of Carrington, until the race died out in 1749, all the male line being extinct, and the property dispersed to remote cousins in the female line.

CARRINGTON CONTINUED

"But there were still Smiths to be found, and no where so thick as in Nottingham, where was situated one of the oldest iron industries in England. From Nottingham sprang a line of prosperous Smiths, who made money and came to London as Bankers about 1780. Of these was Mr. Robert Smith, a gentleman whose whole mind, and latterly his life was engrossed with the earnest longing for a pedigree with Norman blood trickling through it, and so Smith history repeats itself. With infinite pains he traces the family back—taking a lot for granted—to one John Smith of Nottingham about 1660. He found among the old Ashby Folville Smiths who became Carringtons, one John Smith, who had not stooped to participate in the fraud. This John he rolled up into one with his own humble John of Nottingham, and although John Smith of the Ashby Folville family had no surviving issue, he merely discovered that this was an error, and fastened on to him the children of John of Nottingham. He secured a peerage and became Baron Carrington. He left a condition in his will, directing his son to assume by Royal license the surname of Carrington, and so the Norman but purely mythical house of Carrington again adorned the peerage. To make assurance doubly sure, the second Baron bought the chancel of the Ashby Folville church,

which, with the old Smith and Smith-Carrington monuments, he restored, and added a monument to his father, to the collection, presenting a peal of bells and a Communion Service in memory of his adopted ancestors.

"This was the last straw, however, and his first cousin, Augustus Smith, Esq., M.P., for Nottingham, could stand it no longer. He wrote a family history of the Nottingham Smiths, descended from the honest and plebeian John Smith, blacksmith of that town in 1660. He glorified in the fact, and proved not only that the simple blacksmith was an utterly different man from John of the Ashby Folville family, but that the one was dead before the other was born (which is of course a trifle in making a pedigree). Finally he exposed the falsity of the old forged confession of the original John Smith, and poured over that sacred parchment the vials of his wrath and sarcasm. The indignation of his cousin, the Baron Carrington, knew no bounds. His title could not be changed, and he could not now revert to his proper name of Smith. The restored Ashby Folville Church and Monuments remained a monument forever of his family folly.

"The shock to the Peerage editors was severe. The great red book now contains no Carrington fable, and the way it is put is beautiful to those who know the facts.

"Time, however, mellows all things, and only twenty years ago that blatant humbug, Doctor Coppinger of Manchester, produced with the usual flourish a book entitled *The History and Records of the Smith-Carrington Family, from the Conquest to the Present Time*. It was tersely and sarcastically reviewed on its publication as follows: 'This magnificent looking work weights almost 17 lbs. It is accompanied by a genealogical chart, measuring 10 ft. 8 in. by 3 ft. 9 in., requiring a separate case for its accommodation, this is not included in the weight above named. It has been issued at the price of L5 5s. 0d. nett., f. o. r. or steamer.' So whenever you hear of the name Carrington, be it Marquis, Earl, Knight or Baronet, bold warrior, Ambassador or Royal Nurseryman and seedsman, alone or be it linked to Smith as Smith-Carrington or Carrington-Smith, remember the authentic tale I have told you of the great Smith-Carrington Fraud."

William Cowper, in his poem *The Task* rails against the smiths who made weapons:

"Soon, by a righteous judgment, in the line
Of his descending progeny was found
The first artificer of death; the shrewd
Contriver who first sweated at the forge,
And forc'd the blunt and yet unbloodied steel
To a keen edge, and made it bright for war.
Him, Tubal nam'd, the Vulcan of old times,
The sword and falchion their inventor claim;
And the first smith was the first murd'rer's son."

Another viewpoint is expressed by H. D. Smith in his genealogy, *The Smith Family*. He said, "So we may be quite sure that the roots of our genealogical tree must be sought for between the forge and the anvil, in the blacksmith's shop; an origin as honest, if not as honorable, as that of those who have descended from the mailed cutthroats who employed the *Smiths* to make their armor."

SMITH AND ANONYMOUS OFTEN SYNONYMOUS

Few will deny that there are both advantages and disadvantages in bearing the name of Smith. Mr. Smith and Mr. Anonymous, that prolific writer, are almost the same person. A letter sent to Mr. John Smith without a street address would be as likely to arrive as one addressed to the wife of the Man in the Moon. The ubiquitous and sempiternal Smiths have been called nameless, having only a generic appellation. The term *homo sapiens* covers scarcely more ground.

Perhaps the greatest source of irritation to one named Smith is the constant confusion of identity. A Smith is always receiving mail belonging to a brother Smith or being called from his bathtub to the phone only to explain to the caller that he is not the Smith wanted. For instance the author while on board ship was awakened early one morning to explain that he was not the Smith who was scheduled to leave the boat at that time. Again, when the author had been a freshman in college only a few days, he was called to the phone and asked if he was a Mr. Smith, President of a certain organization, and, thinking it was a prank of other students, said no, that he was the owner of the Ritz Hotel. The sudden and contemptuous hanging up of the receiver convinced him that levity was neither called for nor appreciated. Every Smith can tell of many embarrassing experiences when he was mistaken for another.

In a hospital in Cleveland, Ohio, in 1927, three Smtih babies were born at about the same time. Mr. and Mrs. Sam Smith were given a girl baby but claimed they had a boy baby. The other two Smiths said they were satisfied.

Every Smith must bear up under the pseudo-humor of the would-be wit who, upon ascertaining that the name is Smith, says in a mock-serious tone, "Now where have I heard that name before?" The poor, provincial boob never seems to realize that every Smith has smiled rather lamely at that bright remark so many times that he feels that murder is not such a breach of etiquette as is popularly believed. George A. Chase once wrote, in reference to the Smiths, "I am personally acquainted with a number of gentlemen by that name who are honest, conscientious and, according to my notion, very agreeable gentlemen, one of which you can at any time spit on."

The very mention of John Smith in a court-house, police station or other public place brings a broad grin onto everyone's face. One with an uncommon name seeing it in the paper charged with murder, robbery, larceny, arson, mayhem, or some other crime immediately gets very excited and makes all sorts of futile gestures to show his acquaintances and others that he is not the person meant. But any newspaper will relate that Mr. Smith murdered another, robbed a poor widow, assaulted his landlord, set fire to his neighbor's house, stole money from the bank where he worked, beat his wife, fired a church, committed bigamy, picked another's pockets and abused children and every other Smith will be as unconcerned as everyone else.

Every day the newspapers will describe Mr. Smith's charity to the poor, his speech in Congress, his new invention, his opinion on winning the peace, his election to the presidency of a prominent organization, his visit to Queen Elizabeth, his success in the stock market, his sickness, his death, his birth, his marriage, his successful book, his discovery of a cure for a dread disease, and his many other fine accomplishments, which will be read by the other Smiths without the slightest trace of emotion.

THE GREATEST MEN

Truly, Smith is the greatest man in the world. Who is that man who has fought the most battles, made the most speeches, held the most offices, preached the most sermons, performed the most operations, conducted the most lawsuits, sold the most merchandise, sang the most songs, kissed the most girls, and has, in fact, done more of everything than any other person. The answer is clear. You say, we say, and everybody says—Mr. Smith. And history echoes back the same answer.

Even though the name is as common as boiled cabbage it has its good points. It is easy to pronounce, easy to spell, not too long nor too short, easy to write quickly, and one which is not ordinarily confused with other names. These qualities will be appreciated more when we look at some other names. Take for instance, Szczepankiewiecz, found in the Chicago Telephone Directory. How do you pronounce it? How do you spell it? Try writing it quickly and

legibly in a short space on the average form to be filled out for any
reason. If you saw it written, would you recognize it when it is
prounced? Taking all these things into consideration, Smith seems
a pretty good name after all.

A writer in the *Weekly Standard* of East London, South Africa,
said that, considering the number of persons who assume the name
to hide their identity when engaged in some nefarious business, it is
not surprising that anyone owning the name of Smith is looked upon,
on first making his acquaintance, with more or less suspicion. Is he a
real, true born Smith? one is inclined to ask oneself, or is he a
MacGregor, or a Cohen, or a Murphy, or a Jones, merely hiding his
identity for some reason and masquerading as a respectable Smith?
The name of Smith is truly a perpetual incognito.

One John Smith wrote an article in *The Galaxy* in 1876 entitled,
The Inconvenience of Being Named Smith. He did not appear to
have much of a sense of humor and bewailed what he thought was his
misfortune long and loud. Parts of his discourse are sufficiently interesting to quote here. After telling how his college career was
ruined by his sensitiveness to his name, he continued:

"If in travelling I make myself agreeable to a gentleman who at
parting solicits my name, and I tell him, 'Sir!' he is apt to exclaim,
with some impatience, 'I was in earnest, and wished to continue the
acquaintance.' "

INCONVENIENCES OF BEING SMITH

"A young lady once said to me at a large reception, 'As soon as you entered the room, my aunt wondered who you were; and I replied, Mr. Smith, of course; for you know where two or three are gathered together *he* is sure to be.' Had she stopped there I should have been content; but when she added, 'You looked less like him than any gentleman in the room,' I had a spurious sort of feeling, as though I had been detected in imposture, and no doubt looked as pale and limp as a counterfeit greenback. When I have been presented to ladies who had not first been advised of the impending calamity, they have frequently treated the introduction as a joke, and at once began to annoy me by insisting upon knowing my real name."

*   *   *   *   *

"Everybody has known those who would impale a friend on the point of a joke, but it was left for me to have a kinsman who for his own amusement would make a holocaust of his family—one who, like Saturn, would devour his own flesh. My cousin, I thought very hospitably, invited me to spend a fortnight with him in New York. Soon after my arrival he carefully sought all the reputable Smiths of his acquaintance who were unknown to each other, and invited them to meet me at an evening party. I, knowing nothing of the trick, was all affability and smiles to the first ten or twenty of his guests; but as they continued to pour in, my indignation began to arise. I looked narrowly at my host, but his face was grave as the front of a tomb. The guests all round seemed flushed and embarrassed. Men were shaking hands with compliments on their lips and curses in their hearts. Another party approached our host: 'Mr. Smith, Mr. Smith, Mr. Smith, Mr. Smith!'—till the whole room hissed with aspirates like a serpent's den. There is nothing which angers the unfortunate like ridicule. In my native village there was an epileptic so doubled and twisted by disease, that nearly all human likeness was lost. One day a travelling mendicant, whose misfortunes were not unlike his own, came wriggling into town, and, each supposing the other mocked him, they rushed into a tiger-like embrace. In my friend's parlor Smith glared at Smith, each believing himself the victim of a practical joke, but suppressing his rage out of deference to the occasion, and vowing vengeance for the morrow. Still other arrivals, but my kinsman, no longer able to control his spirits, broke into a roar which the silence of the rest of us made ring through the halls like the laugh of a maniac. When he had made his apology and introduced the cheery and ebullient widow Cliquot—the only widow I ever liked—we drowned our vexation and entered grimly into the joke."

* * * * *

"The name is as generic as horse or swan. Let the reader pause and think of it for one moment. It suggests no distinct image, brings up no individual man or woman. Now let him think of Mill or Spurgeon, and a great political economist or popular preacher rises before him; and yet the greatest political economist and the most brilliant divine ever known in Great Britain were both named Smith."

* * * * *

"Praise a Frenchman in public, and somebody present will wriggle and shrug his shoulders. Abuse an Englishman, and someone will growl and get red in the face; but you can abuse a Smith in any assembly, and though the particular one you mean may be present, nobody's feelings are hurt. You may flatter him and offend no man's modesty. There is no common sympathy in the family. Strangers meeting who have any other name in common feel an interest in each other, and at once set about discovering a connection between their families; but a Smith who would do this would only be laughed at for his folly."

* * * * *

"We put premiums upon the heads of catamounts and wolves, but let the Smiths go free. I do not know that I would have a price set on their scalps, but they should have the largest possible liberty to get rid of themselves."

"It will surprise the Smiths to learn how easily their names may be changed. A wriggle a shiver, and a hop, and the tadpole leaps into a frog; and by a process just as simple a Smith may become a Buckingham. No sprinkling with water, no laying on of hands, no special statute, no judicial decree, is necessary; he has only to declare his purpose by publishing a newspaper advertisement, by changing the sign over his place of business, or by any other means he may see fit to employ. 'This is a free country, and a man may spell as he pleases,' said a late Congreeman who spelled onion with a *u*.' "

Of the Smiths it might be truly said, in the words of Fitz-Greene Halleck:

"For thou art Freedom's now, and Fame's;
One of the few, the immortal names,
That were not born to die."

CHAPTER 8

The Smiths Of Old

AMONG the most primitive peoples there was very little division of labor. Each man manufactured his own garments, weaving the cloth from materials obtained in the forests. He provided his family with meat by hunting wild animals. The women cultivated the land to provide grain and vegetables. Chickens and goats were tended by the children. Each man made his own bows, bowstrings and the shafts for his arrows, but he had to depend upon the village smith for arrow- and spear-heads, knives and crude bracelets.

The smith was paid for his services with the necessities of life, such as meat, fowls, herbs, and palm cloth.

IMPORTANCE IN THE COMMUNITY

So the smith was an important person in the community as soon as the metal age started. The earliest craftsmen were in the metal trades. Among most early peoples the smith was of great consequence, although it is curious to note that in some countries he was regarded as a servant or even slave of the entire village—as in the early Greek villages, and in many villages in Africa.

The whole foundation of civilized life, all its necessities, comforts, conveniences and pleasures, from the earliest times, depended on the smith. That the art of the smith is one of the first essentials to any civilization is beyond question. Mention of its founder, Tubal Cain, mentioned in the Scriptures, is deserving of a place with the other great inventors.

So important was the trade of the smith in ancient warfare that conquerors often removed them from a vanquished nation to disable it. The Philistines deprived the Hebrews of their smiths.

In 1 *Sam. xiii,* 19, where we are told, "Now there was no smith found throughout all the land of Israel." Nebuchadnezzar, king of Babylon, so treated them in later times, (2 *Kings,* xxiv, 14; *Jer.* xxiv, 1; xxix, 2). Herodotus tells us that Cyrus controlled the Lydians in much the same manner.

An old proverb declares, "By the hammer and hand all the arts do stand." This may seem to be a broad statement, but if we examine some of the more elaborate arts, we shall be more impressed with the truth of the ancient saying. As an example, we can look at textile fabrics. They are the products of looms, of course. But the hammer was used in the construction of the looms, and earlier than that there were other machines, of one kind or another, in which the hammer played an even more important part, until finally we reach a point where the hammer and hand laid the very foundation of the industry. We would have to go back to this point if all our machines were suddenly blotted out of existence. Thus, both the hammer and hand had everything to do with the creation of all other arts. From this point of view the dignity and importance of the smith's art is at once apparent. Everyone must go to the smith for his hammer. The smith alone, of all workers, enjoys the distinction of producing his own tools. The hammer has been properly called the king of tools.

SOLOMON AND THE SMITH

The legend of King Solomon illustrates the importance of the worker at the forge in early times.

When Solomon, the Son of David, had finished the Temple in Jerusalem he invited all the chief architects, the important artificers, the cunning workers in gold, wood, ivory, and stone, all the important men who had helped in the building of the sacred temple, to a great dinner, saying, "Sit down. I have prepared a great feast for all the cunning artificers. Stretch forth your hands. For is not the laborer worthy of his hire? Is not the artificer worthy of his honor?" When everyone was seated and before they had started to eat and drink, a knock was heard at the door, and a man burst into the room. "Who are you?" cried the angry Solomon. The stranger replied, "When men deride me they call me the Smith, but when they wish to honor me, I am called the Son of the Forge. Smith is not inapt, and your servant desires no better name." Then, asked Solomon, "Why have you come so rudely and uninvited to my feast when only the chief builders of the Temple were invited?" Replied the man, "Please, my Lord, your servants tried to prevent me from entering, but I came not unbidden. Was it not proclaimed that all the chief

workmen of the Temple were called to this feast?" Then he who
raised the walls said, "He is no cutter in stone." And he who made
the roof cried out, "He is not skilled in cedar wood, neither does he
know how to join great pieces of timber together." The man who
inlaid the great building with fine gold said, "Neither is he a worker
in precious metals." One who carved the cherubim said, "He is no
sculptor." Solomon turned to the man, "What have you to say
Smith? Why shouldn't I order you to be put to death?" The Son of
the Forge was not dismayed. Standing before the king he exclaimed,
"Oh King, live forever. The workers here have said that I am not of
them and they are right. Before they were able to do their work, I
had to do mine. I am their master." And he turned around and said
to each of them, "Who made the tools with which you work?" And
each one answered, "The Smith." "Enough, good fellow,"
proclaimed the King, "You have proved that you were invited. Go
and wash the smut of the forge from your face and come and sit at
my right hand. You are the greatest of all the Temple workers."

Similar legends about the smiths are told concerning other kings.

THE SMITH IN AFRICA

Mircea Eliade, in his *The Forge and the Crucible,* observes that
among many African tribes the legend of the First Smith, the
Civilizing Hero, was widespread. This First Smith came down to
earth and revealed not only fire and the means of preparing food by
cooking but also the art of building houses, the art of hunting, the
sexual behavior necessary for procreation, the technique of giving
birth, circumcision, forms of burial, and, indeed, all useful
techniques.

The smith's tools were originally made of stone. This is shown by
the frequency with which their names are derived from the old
Indo-Germanic word for stone. Even though the smith worked in
metals, they were far too scarce and valuable to be used in making
tools when stone implements could be used instead.

In ancient Egypt the smith is found very early. A scribe of the
Twelfth Dynasty (2000-1788 B.C.) advised young men to enter a
profession rather than a trade. Of the smith he said, "I have never
seen a blacksmith on an embassy, nor a smelter sent on a mission,

but I have seen the smith at his work—at the mouth of the furnace of his forge—his fingers as rugged as the hide of a crocodile, and stinking more than fish spawn."

In Greece the crafts began to emerge in the four or five centuries between the fall of Troy and the early part of the sixth century B.C. Even then the smith's forge, like the country stores and smithies of the small towns of our own times, was the place where all the idlers and gossips of the village congregated. The legendary Chalybes were a nation of smiths.

In Italy, iron was known over a thousand years before Christ. In that region, the men of the Bronze Age were highly skilled in the working of that metal, so from the first discovery of iron they became proficient with it. Many smith shops have been unearthed at Pompeii, some containing both tools and finished products.

Throughout Old Testament times the traveling smith went from one community to another, stopping wherever his skill was required to make cooking utensils, vessels for the wine press, tools for farmers and masons, and shoes for horses. Without him the civilization of the Hebrews would have been much more primitive.

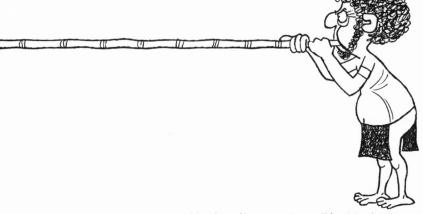

Many smiths are also found in the tribes of Africa. The Macheva in East Africa are the most expert workers in iron, and the smiths are often the chiefs of their villages. The pygmies made spears from iron found in the forests to sell to other tribes. In other tribes in Africa the smith occupies a special position among the people. In some tribes they are slaves and outcasts, but they are regarded everywhere as necessary to the life of the people. In the Western Sudan smiths are held in high esteem and consort with princes and kings.

No village in India is without its smith. At the festival of the Doorga in Benares a smith, chosen because of his strength, kills a buffalo with a single stroke of a knife and its head is presented to the idol. The animal must fall under one blow, otherwise the omen would be deemed most unfortunate and the sacrificer would be driven away from the place with scorn and cursing. If he succeeds, he is hailed as a great benefactor of the country. Among the Buryat tribesmen of Asia smiths are regarded as close relatives of the gods.

In Germany skillful smiths were held in the highest esteem. In ancient Germanic times the trade of a smith was the only one in which a free man could engage without degrading himself. Many of the early German heroes added to their fame by making their own weapons and shields. During the middle ages in Germany there were public smithies open to all, and each man forged whatever he needed.

As Spain was the greatest metalliferous country of antiquity, we find the smiths there very skillful and of high standing in the community. The workers in iron were artists of the highest rank and the amazing grandeur and design of their ironwork has never been equalled by any other country.

In Finland the respect for the smiths is shown by the old proverb:

"Fine bread always for the smith,
Dainty morsels for the hammerer."

Even today they are held in the highest esteem.

IN THE BRITISH ISLES

In Ireland and Scotland the smith and his work were highly respected as shown by the frequent use of the name in their topography. Thus there is Ardgowan (the smith's height), Balgowan, Balnagowan, Balgownie, Balgonie, in Scotland; and Ballygow, Ballygowan, Ballingown, Ballynagown in Ireland (the dwelling of the smith). It was considered an additional distinction for a chief or warrior to be a good smith. The ancient Brehon law tracts of Ireland recognized the importance of. the smith and carefully defined his rights and privileges.

A story is told of a Highland smith who had committed a crime and needed to be punished. But since the chief could not dispense with the smith, he offered to hang two weavers in his place. Among Highland clans the smith ranked third in dignity to the chief.

That the smiths were important persons in ancient Wales is shown by the number of times they are mentioned in the Venedotian, Dimetian, and Gwentian codes, for North, South, and Southeast Wales respectively. These codes were compiled by order of Howel, the Good, in the early part of the tenth century. In these laws there were three arts which a villein could not teach his son without first obtaining the permission of the lord—scholarship, smithcraft and bardism.

SPECIAL PRIVILEGES

A smith was one of the officers of the court and had many privileges especially enumerated in the laws, among which were the right to have the heads and feet of the cattle slaughtered in the palace; victuals for himself and his servant from the palace; free land; lawful liquor from the palace; the same mill privileges as the king; the right to heriots (the best beast or chattel paid upon death) from the smiths under him and fees upon the marriage of their daughters. In return for this he was to do all the king's work free except for the cauldron, broad axe and spear head. He could collect a fee of four pence for putting prisoners in irons and liberating them.

In the early Welsh laws there were three ornaments of a hamlet, a book, a teacher versed in song, and a smith in his smithy. The meaning of the term *smithcraft* was more comprehensive than it is today. The smith must have united different branches of knowledge which are now practiced separately, such as raising the ore, converting it into metal, and shaping it into weapons, armor, etc. Part of his profession was to teach young warriors how to use the weapons he made for them.

During Anglo-Saxon times the smith was a person of consequence. In the courts of the Anglo-Saxon kings he was a man of considerable distinction and his privileges exceeded those of any other craftsman, where he was ranked even above the physician. Early Anglo-Saxon laws mentioned the smith many times. His importance is not surprising when we consider the many small villages scattered over a large area, each with a church, a smith's shop and a market place forming, respectively, the religious, social and economic center of the community.

Each village and district had to be self-supporting in those days when traveling was difficult and dangerous because of bad roads and the insecurity of life and property. The ordinary use of metal in everyday life made the smith an important adjunct to the community, and the dependence upon him for arms and armor caused him to be treated as an officer of the highest rank. He made and repaired the weapons used in war, on the temper and quality of which life, honor, and victory in battle depended. Every knight had at least one smith, or armorer, in his employ.

This general reputation of the smith was recognized by Longfellow in his *Evangeline* when he wrote:

> For since the birth of time, throughout all ages and nations,
> Has the craft of the smith been held in repute by the people.

Since the smith was of such great importance, many stories were told concerning him and his work. One legend dates from about 700 A.D. Alcester, in Warwickshire, England, was the center of busy ironworks, peopled with smiths, who, for their hardness of heart in refusing to listen to St. Egwin and drowning his voice by beating on their anvils, were swallowed up by the earth. Afterwards, as a punishment by God, no smith was able to ply his trade successfully at Alcester.

ST. DUNSTAN

Just before the Norman Conquest some of the clergy labored in the mechanical arts. It was even required by law that the clergy be required to pursue such occupations. Under this stimulus many learned smithcraft and made ornaments for the church. As this was

the most highly regarded work, it was to be expected that the churchmen would prefer it over other possible endeavors.

St. Dunstan, who died in 988 A.D., was a favorite with King Athelstan, whom he pleased by his performances on the harp. St. Dunstan was a smith. He passed a quiet life working at his forge in a small cell. One legend says that the devil often tempted and annoyed St. Dunstan. On one of his visits, the Saint, while working at his forge, seized the devil's nose with the red-hot tongs and forced him to sign a promise never to molest Holy Church or Holy men, and to keep aloof from all buildings in which hang the horseshoe. A similar legend is told of St. Eloi. Even today we consider the horseshoe an emblem of good luck, especially when hung over the entrance of a building.

The importance of the smithy in the minds of the people is illustrated in a semi-Saxon manuscript of the thirteenth century called *The Ancren Riwle*, a treatise on the rules and duties of monastic life, where it says, *"Al þes world is Goddes Smiððe, worte smeoðien his icorene. Wultu þet God nabbe no fur in his smiððe—ne belies—ne homeres?"* In modern English that means, "All this world is God's smithy, in which he forgeth his elect. Wouldst thou that God had no fire in his smithy, nor bellows, nor hammers?"

As the Anglo-Saxons were a warlike people, the field of honor was the battlefield and a valorous soldier or brave leader was referred to as a battle-smith. Thus in the *Anglo-Saxon Chronicle,* compiled about 938 A.D., we find the following:

> "since hither came
> from the eastern shores
> the Angles and Saxons,
> over the broad sea,
> and Britain sought,—
> fierce battle-smiths,
> o'ercame the Welsh,
> most valiant earle,
> and gained the land."

Evidence of the influence of the smith and his work in Anglo-Saxon times is shown by the poetical combinations of the word in ancient Anglo-Saxon literature, some of which date back to the beginning of the eighth century.

In the Anglo-Saxon poem, *The Legend of St. Andrew,* written the latter part of the tenth century, fierce grynsmiths (evil-smiths or evildoers) are mentioned. In the same poem wrohtsmiths (workers of crime or criminals) are noted. They are also found in *The Legend of Saint Guthlac.* This tale also mentions teonsmiths, which is translated as workers of hurt or wrong.

But not all of these compounds of the word have negative meanings. In *Caedmon's Metrical Paraphrase* we find a reference to laughtersmiths, which must be the forerunner of our modern jokesmiths. The Anglo-Saxon poem *Elene* speaks of larsmiths, which means wise smiths or counsellors. The reference to the wigsmiths, or warriors, is from the *Anglo-Saxon Chronicle.* In the *Liber Psalmorum* (Anglo-Saxon Paraphrase of the Psalms) wigsmiths are found to mean idol-smiths or makers of idols. In *Beowulf* a wondersmith, or mystic smith, is mentioned.

Even Vulcanus is defined as the fire god, or hellsmith, in one of the early Anglo-Saxon glossaries. The devil has also been called Hellsmith. Early Anglo-Saxon laws mention the king's ambiht-smith, meaning official smith. Many other compounds familiar to us today are found in Anglo-Saxon literature, such as *arsmith* (coppersmith or brass worker), *isensmith* (ironsmith or blacksmith), *goldsmith,* and *seolforsmith* (silversmith).

In the Old Norse we find *ljoðasmiðr,* verse-smith. It has been observed that since the name of Smith was given to anyone who smites, calling a poet a verse-smith was all right as he cudgels his brain. Old Norse mythology describes Loki as a mischief-smith. Coming down to the present day we find the poem by Erik Axel Karlfeldt, which, in translation is entitled *The Rhymesmith.*

WITH WILLIAM THE CONQUEROR

The victory of William the Conqueror at Hastings in 1066 was attributed by him largely to the superior weapons of his men and he exalted the smith to a rank equal to the highest official. From the Conquest on, the importance of the craft of the smith as a maker of arms and armor can scarcely be overestimated. It was largely due to the development of weapons and defensive armor that we owe much of the great improvement of art and craftmanship in England and, indeed, all over Europe.

A guild of London goldsmiths existed as early as 1180, and in 1327 the goldsmiths were regularly incorporated in England. "The Articles of the Blacksmiths," dated 1372, are enrolled in the Guildhall records. The work of the smith was significant in building up the huge iron manufacturing trade of England, an important early source of the wealth of the British Empire.

IN EARLY AMERICA

Almost every city or village in America can look back to the time when its "business district" consisted of a general store and a blacksmith's shop. The blacksmith's shop was often built first, since it was an essential part of pioneer life. In many places it vied with the general store and post office as a place where the villagers congregated when not working. We know that in England the smithy

was a gathering place for the idle of the village because the slang term, "smithy-chat," a phrase meaning gossip from the smithy, is still often heard in many rural sections of England.

DECLINE OF IMPORTANCE

In modern times the smith's work has so declined that beautiful ironwork by the smith has become almost obsolete, and he is today regarded as little better than the ordinary laborer. The old worker in iron produced pieces which are not easy to copy, such as slotting a bar, so as to get the eyes at equal distances, without a machine; or cutting slits into a bar from the edge, and curling the splintered parts. This was common work for the smith of the twelfth century. Machines have today so relegated the smith to the background that when we now need good examples of ironwork, as required in some styles of architecture, we return to our old models. We imitate the good, honest work of our forefathers who, with a few primitive tools, produced such beauty of form as is not found today.

This decrease in the importance of the smith started as early as the beginning of the seventeenth century in England. The art was stimulated somewhat by the reconstruction work necessary after the great London fire in 1666, but this was only temporary. The skill of the smith began to decline in other European countries about this time.

The smith's work was further reduced by the use of castings which began in the eighteenth century, and became quite extensive because they were much cheaper than wrought iron although not nearly as beautiful. Again, an act of Parliament prohibited the use of those elaborate and ornamental signs we associate with old London. This was almost as serious a blow to the smith as the use of castings. The gradual, general use of coal as fuel did away with fire dogs, grids, spits, and many other items which formed a very basic portion of the smith's business. The stove took the place of the old picturesque fireplace, which in turn was replaced by modern steam, gas and electric heaters. The increasing use of machinery has helped make the true smith almost extinct and smithcraft is today well nigh a lost art.

In early times the smith was a real artist, as the beautiful specimens of his remaining handiwork show. Doors, hinges, knockers, railings, andirons, grilles protecting tombs, gates, handrails, and other examples of the smith's work, are found in large numbers in the early churches and museums of Europe. The smith's heart was in his work then and his object was not to finish a job as quickly as possible, but to execute it in fine style.

HISTORY AND IMPORTANCE OF IRON

As the history of the ancient smiths is so closely bound up with that of iron, it is important here to take a look at the history of iron in the world. This common metal is not only the most widely distributed in the world, but it is also the most valuable. It is the keystone of civilization. To quote from John Locke, "Were the use of iron lost among us, we should in a few ages be unavoidably reduced to the wants and ignorance of the ancient savage Americans; so that he who first made known the use of that contemptible mineral may be truly styled the father of Arts and the author of Plenty." When Croesus was displaying his great treasures of gold to Solon, it is said that, upon conclusion of the exhibition, Solon remarked, "If another comes that hath better iron than you, he will be master of all that gold." The strength and wealth of nations is dependent upon iron far more than upon gold.

Iron was one of the last metals to come into general use, because it is seldom found, except in the case of meteorites, in anything like the form we know it. To recognize its ores requires more skill and observation than is possessed by most primitive peoples. One unacquainted with the metal would never recognize it in the earth, and a high degree of heat is required to fuse it.

We do not know who first applied fire to ore to make it workable. It was probably accidentally discovered in different places at different times through the chance association of ore and a hot fire. It is not even known who first started to use furnaces in connection with metals, nor the use of bellows to make the fire hotter. For best results iron must be combined in varying proportions with other substances, but when that is done it can be used for purposes as diverse as a pin and a railroad engine, a surgeon's lancet and a steam hammer, the mainspring of a watch and a suspension bridge.

Gold, on the other hand, is found pure and in an almost workable state, so in very early times was much more plentiful than iron or steel, but was not suited for the purpose of tools, weapons, or armor. It was too soft to serve for a saw, axe, or sword, while tempered steel would serve all these purposes. For this reason we find many early warring nations, where iron was scarce, making the handles and backs of their swords of gold or copper, and economizing on the more practical metal, iron, to form the cutting edge. This is particularly true in the ancient Scandinavian countries. Caesar relates that iron was produced in such small quantities along the coast of Britain that it was considered a precious metal and iron bars of specified weights were used by the Britons as money.

Before the Iron Age in archaeology most peoples passed through an age characterized by the use of alloys of copper and tin, known as the Bronze Age, which lasted until iron began to be used for tools and weapons. Stone was used in this age alongside copper and bronze due to the scarcity of metals. Iron gradually came into use, and there is no well-defined line between the Bronze Age and the Iron Age. The Iron Age is not commonly regarded as starting until the use of that metal was widespread.

The oldest piece of wrought iron in existence is about 5,000 years old, and was found in one of the Egyptian pyramids. A few other early specimens have also been found. Despite this, many authorities claim that iron was not clearly used there before about 800 B.C. The earliest iron objects were weapons and ornaments, not tools, which had to wait until the metal was more plentiful.

Some writers have attempted to explain the failure to find iron objects among ancient remains by pointing out the tendency of iron to rust away quickly. This explanation does not appear to be sound because even if rust did attack the metal, it would not cause the object to disappear without a trace. Also, many of the remains unearthed have been in places secure from moisture where oxidation would be exceedingly slow.

The oldest description of the use of iron in China appears in the *Yu Kung,* and dates from 2200 B.C. In Babylon a document written about 2000 B.C. mentions iron, but it was then extremely rare. In India there is evidence of the manufacture of iron as early, at least, as 2000 B.C., although the Iron Age did not begin there until about 1370 B.C. The Hittites began working the iron ore deposits along the Black Sea before the thirteenth century B.C. In Greece and Italy the use of iron dates from about 900 B.C. although there have been miscellaneous finds of the metal attributable to a period several centuries earlier. The Bible contains numerous references to iron.

A very ancient industry in metals had its seat near the Danube and in Spain. These centers became so important that the Romans themselves, under their first emperors, imported their finest weapons from these countries, otherwise so generally despised by those haughty people.

About the middle of the nineteenth century many objects characteristic of the first iron age of Central and Western Europe were found near Hallstatt in Upper Austria. Due to the importance of this discovery, the first iron age in archaeology is now known as the Hallstatt period extending from about 900 to 400 B.C. Objects found in these ancient graves at Hallstatt are among the earliest evidence of the work in iron in Europe.

Iron was first introduced into Britain about the end of the fifth, or the beginning of the fourth, century before the Christian era. About the year 120 A.D. the Romans had forges in the West of England, both in the Forest of Dean and in South Wales where they made weapons for the troops. Many iron objects found throughout the South and West of England mark the industry of the Romans in the early working of iron. They were probably the first to make iron in any quantity in England and the first to recognize the value of the mineral wealth of the country.

In the eighth century a lot of iron was manufactured in England as well as in Spain, France and Germany. In early times England imported a great deal of iron from Germany and Spain, and even today imports some of the better grades from Norway and Sweden.

Very few iron implements have been found in ancient America, except for a few implements made out of meteoric iron. This paucity of iron was certainly responsible to a large extent for the difference in the state of civilization between the early peoples of the Americas and the natives of Europe. Up to the time the Europeans began to colonize America the natives were still in what is known as the stone age, having little knowledge of metals, with the exception of gold, the metal first discovered and used by most savage peoples. In South America some silver and bronze was used in addition to gold, among the more developed tribes, but even there this absence of a knowledge of iron made them inferior to Europeans. The natives of the Americas were skilled in pottery, which forms the bulk of the important objects found by archaeologists, rather than metal pieces.

SUPERNATURAL POWERS

When metals were first introduced among savage peoples, it is not surprising to find that they regarded with superstitious awe the men who shaped this new and wonderful, almost mysterious, material. The smiths were not slow in noting this and did not hesitate to add magic words and flourishes, the better to impress those who did not share their secrets. In Japan, as elsewhere, they tried to enhance the importance of their art by mystery. There the smith who forged the swords worked alone in his shop while he was finishing the blades and sang and chanted spells which were, it was imagined, wrought at the same time into the metal. This use of magic is especially common in the manufacture of swords, the most important part of the ancient warrior's equipment, often claimed to be the work of supernatural hands.

As the smiths were credited with the highest degree of skill possible to man, it is not difficult to understand that other arts were ascribed to them. Many were thought to be skilled in medicine, as well as music, poetry and dance. Throughout central Asia the belief in the healing powers and salutary knowledge of the smiths is widely diffused.

In many places throughout Europe ancient man was so amazed at the art of molding the hard metal in the fire and fashioning such useful things out of it that its working came to be ascribed to supernatural beings. They could not conceive of mortal beings exercising this art without the assistance of mysterious and magical powers. The ancient Germans characterized these smiths as wily, deceitful and treacherous, and the malevolent smith was used to illustrate the Christian idea of the Evil One. The old Teutonic conceptions of the smith and the devil, both of whom worked with fire, had much in common.

SMITH IN MYTHOLOGY

In Teutonic mythology the dwarfs, known also as elves, are small folk who live underground, and work in stone and metals. The women spin and weave; the men are smiths. To those who are kind to them these dwarfs are very helpful, but care must be taken to place food for them every night. A fairy tale, common to many countries, concerns the dwarf who comes every night to the smithy of one who had been kind to him and does the work, with wondrous skill, that the smith had taken in during the previous day.

According to Netherlandish tradition, there is not a village or hamlet that does not have its dwarf-cave or dwarf-hole. In the forests the remains of ancient smithies are often found, which the people call dwarf-smithies. In Greece and Germany almost identical stories were told of master smiths whose presence was mysteriously concealed from the sight of the village inhabitants. In the morning a man out riding heard some smiths at work and cried out that he wished they would make him a chaff-knife. Upon his return he found it and paid the proper amount of money. Wounds caused by it were said to be unhealable. Invisible water-smiths are also mentioned. This kind of story about smiths working in secret is found in Sir Walter Scott's *Kenilworth*.

Some writers have expressed the belief that dwarfs, so often mentioned in the ancient sagas and fairy tales, were real beings, probably the Phoenician miners, who, working the iron, copper, gold and tin mines took advantage of the credulity of the early inhabitants to make them believe that they belonged to a supernatural race that lived underground in a region called *Svart-alfa-heim*, or the home of the black elves.

SMITH AND THE DEVIL

The best-known fairy tales about the smith concern "The Smith and the Devil," and "The Smith and the Fairies." In the former tale a smith made a bargain with the devil, promising to let the fiend have his soul after seven years of prosperity and success. On one of these visits by the devil, the Smith was given three wishes. He wished that anyone who climbed his pear tree could not come down without his consent, that anyone who sat in his chair could not get up without his consent, and that anyone who entered his purse could not leave without his consent. By entrapping the devil in the pear tree and the chair he won two more seven-year periods of life. When the devil came to get him for the third time he induced him to make himself small enough to enter his steel mesh purse. Then he locked the purse,

heated it in the fire and pounded it with his sledgehammer until the devil, shrieking in great pain, promised to leave and never come again. After the smith died the devil, still frightened of him, saw him approach Hell and locked the doors to keep him out. The smith then applied for admission into Heaven, but St. Peter refused him. Thereupon the Smith threw his cloak into the partly opened door and, after being allowed to go in to recover it, sat down and refused to budge.

WIZARDRY OF THE SMITH

In Abyssinia it is said that all smiths are looked upon as wizards. They are generally credited with the ability to turn themselves into hyenas and other wild beasts, so that few people will molest a blacksmith. As for offending a blacksmith, most people even in this country are hesitant to do that and for a good reason, as Longfellow noted.

> "The smith, a mighty man is he,
>   With large and sinewy hands;
> And the muscles of his brawny arms
>   Are strong as iron bands."

Around such an important and mysterious craft as that of the smith, most peoples, from the earliest times, have tended to weave the stories of their gods and legendary heroes. Mythology and folklore refer constantly to the smith. The genealogy of the smiths, like that of royalty, goes back to the gods. A short sketch of each of the most important smith-gods and legendary heroes is arranged here in alphabetical order.

SMITH AND THE FAIRIES

In "The Smith and the Fairies" a Smith lived who had a son about thirteen years old. The boy became very ill and for a long time his health did not improve. The Smith went to a wise man who told him that the fairies had his son, having put a changeling in his place. Following the wise man's instructions, the Smith proved the invalid to be a changeling by carrying egg shells full of water before it and drawing out the exclamation, "I am 800 years old, and I never saw

such a thing before." The Smith then got rid of the changeling by throwing it into a hot fire and it bounded up through a hole in the roof with a loud yell. Then, upon the advice of the wise man, the Smith went to the fairies' hill, on a night when it was open, to rescue his son, taking with him a Bible, a dirk and a crowing cock. Sticking the dirk into the opening he prevented the fairies from closing it. With the Bible in his hands they could not harm him. When the Smith requested his son, the fairies gave such a loud laugh that the cock, dozing peacefully under the Smith's coat, was awakened and began to crow. This so irritated the fairies that they threw both the Smith and his son out. Back at the Smith's forge the son did not speak for a year and a day, but just sat in the corner with dull and unseeing eyes. Then one day when the Smith was making a sword which was not turning out as well as he wished, his son suddenly took it from him and, plying the tools with great skill, fashioned a far better sword than the Smith had ever seen before. From then on the son worked constantly with his father, producing such wonderful work that the whole countryside went to them to have their work done, and both grew rich and lived a happy, useful life together.

These two stories are found in the folk-lore of a great many countries, with variations characteristic of the different cultures.

SMITH GODS AND HEROES

AZAZEL was a sort of evil supernatural power. In the apocalyptic *Enoch* we read, "And Azazel taught men to make swords and knives and shields, and coats of mail, and made known to them metals and the art of working them, bracelets, and ornaments, and the use of antimony, and the beautifying of the eyebrows, and the most costly and the choicest stones and all colouring tinctures, so that the world was changed." This change was not regarded as for the better, since the writer then proceeded to relate how there then arose great godlessness, sin and corruption.

BELKAN, the Assyrian fire-god, was identified with Vulcan.

CREIDNE was an Irish god who made rivets for the spears, hilts for the swords and bosses and rims for the shields. He is said to have been drowned while bringing golden ore from Spain to Ireland.

CRYSOR was the Phoenician god identified with Vulcan.

CYCLOPES. The Cyclopes were, according to Pliny, the inven-

tors of the art of working iron. There were more than one hundred of them. They worked under Vulcan in the island of Lemnos and forged the helmet for Pluto which made him invisible, and the trident for Neptune among other things.

DEMIAN. See Kuz'ma-Dem'yan.

ECKEHARD, known also as Ecke, Eckenbrecht, and Eckesachs, was, in *Rosengarten,* an old German epic of the thirteenth century, a celebrated weapon-smith. He worked for Mimer.

GIRRU was a Babylonian god of light and fire, equated with Vulcan and Thor, and regarded as the god of smithcraft.

GLAUCUS, of Chios, discovered the art of forging iron, according to Pausanias. Strabo ascribes it to the Idaean Dactyli, and the art of making utensils of bronze and iron to the Telchines; the former were inhabitants of Crete, the latter of Rhodes. Pliny says, "Hesiod says, that iron was discovered in Crete by the Idaean Dactyli."

GOIBNIU was the smith-god of the ancient Irish, and figured in many of their old romances. He made the weapons of the gods promising that no spear-head forged by him would miss, and anyone it pierced would die. His ale preserved one from old age, disease and death.

HEPHAISTOS is the Greek form of the Latin Vulcan.

HERTRICH was a co-worker with Mimer, and the only smith to be compared to him in skill according to some legends. Hertrick assisted Mimer in making all the treasures he produced.

HORUS, an Egyptian god identified with Vulcan, was, among other things, the instructor of smiths and other artificers, adorned with whose tools he often appeared. Horus had a short or lame leg to signify that agriculture or husbandry will halt without the assistance of the smiths.

ILMARINE was "the eternal Smith of the Finns." In the national epic of Finland, *The Kalevala,* he was a famous smith-god who wrought the heavens of blue steel, and did the work so well that neither mark of hammer nor trace of tongs was left upon the sky.

KUZ'MA-DEM'YAN was the divine smith of the early Russians. In later times the name is separated and Kuzma and Demyan are often given as two different saints. This saint is often mentioned in the Russian folk songs of which the following, taken from W. R. Shedden Ralston's translation, is an example:

"There comes a Smith from the forge, *Glory!*
The Smith carried three hammers, *Glory!*
Smith, Smith, forge me a crown, *Glory!*
Forge me a crown both golden and new, *Glory!*
Forge from the remnants a golden ring, *Glory!*
And from the chips a pin, *Glory!*
In that crown will I be wedded, *Glory!*
With that ring will I be betrothed, *Glory!*
With that pin will I fasten the nuptial kerchief, *Glory!*

Many legends are told about this saint. One of them relates how, just after he had made a plow, a great snake attempted to attack him. As soon as it had licked a hole through the smithy, the Saint seized it by the tongue with his pincers—as firmly as St. Dunstan seized the devil—harnessed it to the plow and compelled it to plow the land from sea to sea. The snake vainly prayed for a drink of water from the Dnieper, but the Saint continued to drive it until they came to the Black Sea, where it drank the sea half-dry and then burst. In other legends the Saint passes as a skillful physician.

MIME was a famous smith who was Siegfried's instructor. After him was named the magic sword Miming which was forged by Voland (Wieland) and carried off by Mimir, a Scandinavian giant, uncle of the god Odhin. He was slain by Siegfried. Mime seems to be the same being as Regin.

MIMER, in Norse legend, was the chief smith. In some stories he is the same as Mime, and in others appears to be a different person. Mimer seems to be just another name for Regin. Mimer was said to be the most excellent smith in the world, better even than Wieland (Volund, Wayland). Among his apprentices are mentioned Velint (Volund), Sigurd-Sven (Siefried), and Eckehard. Mimer was the sole possessor of the mythic mead, the magic fountain, from which the gods acquired creative power, wisdom and the desire to accomplish great deeds.

MULCIBER is another name for Vulcan. It is said to be a corruption of *mulcifer* (from *mulceo,* to soften or render tractable, and *ferrum,* iron).

NINIP, also known as Adar and Uras, was a Babylonian god whom the Assyrians worshipped because of their military tendencies.

Ninip was identified with iron under the name Baru or An-bar.

OBERON was the king of the dwarfs and elves. At his command the dwarfs, who were very clever smiths, forged marvelous weapons and fashioned wonderful jewels which he bestowed upon favorite mortals.

PHTHA, or PTAH, was the great god of the people of ancient Memphis, in Egypt. He was the artificer for the Egyptian gods, and so was identified with Vulcan.

REGIN was a treacherous dwarf smith, brother of Fafnir and foster-father of Sigurd (the German Siegfreid). He incited Sigurd to slay Fafnir, told him of the wrongs Fafnir had done him and that he intended to kill him later. Sigurd learned of his purpose and killed him with a sword Regin had made for him. This sword was so sharp that when he thrust it into the Rhine and let a strand of wool float against it, the strand was cut into two pieces. It also cut Regin's great anvil in two without even being dented. In some myths Regin is also represented as being the wisest of men.

SETHLANS was the Etruscan fire-god identified with Vulcan. It is said that he delivered Tinia (Jupiter) of Menrva (Minerva).

SINDRI, in Scandinavian legends, was a dwarf, the most famous of smiths. With his brother Brokkr, he forged the iron mace or hammer, called Mjolnir for Thor, who is usually represented with it in his hand.

TWASHTRI was the smith god of India corresponding in many respects with Hephaistos and Vulcan. In the *Rig*-veda he is represented as the ideal artist, the divine artisan, the most skillful of workmen. He sharpened the great iron axe, and forged the thunderbolts of the fierce Indra. He is the shaper of all forms, human and animal, and creator of the world. Today he is often regarded as the patron deity of artificers.

VULCAN (Greek, Hephaistos) was the Roman god of fire, a celebrated worker in metals and maker of armor. According to Homer he was a son of Zeus (Jupiter) and Hera (Juno), and was

weak and deformed at birth. Others said he was a son of Juno and had no father. Some writers identify him with the Tubal-Cain of Scripture. In a quarrel between Jupiter and Juno he took the part of his mother and was hurled down from Olympus by Jupiter, and, after falling a whole day, he landed on the island of Lemnos, the fall making him lame. He forged the thunderbolts of Jupiter and made the shield of Hercules and the armor of Achilles. He married Venus. His forge was on Mount Etna, but, according to popular tradition, he had workshops in several volcanic islands, and the Cyclopes worked for him. He is represented with hammer and tongs at the anvil and with his right arm bare. Vulcan had a variety of names, most of them referring either to his lameness or the location of his forges. Among them are Aetnaeus, Amphiguneis, Iunonigena, Kullopodios, Lemnius, Lipareus, and Tardipes.

WAYLAND THE SMITH was an early English legendary smith, who, with his brother Egill, probably had his home in the North of England. His name is connected in legends with smiths in southern England and in Westphalia. His story is one of the oldest songs of the *Elder Edda,* and is not later than the beginning of the eighth century. In the Scandinavian languages he is called Volund Volundr, Valand, Velent; in German, Wieland or Eielant, and is represented as having two brothers, Slagfith and Egil.

The above group is only a rough list of the mystical beings who are known in folklore as famous smiths. Besides these gods, many other thunder and firegods were related more or less remotely to the smiths or had the smith's skill. The many resemblances in the stories of the smith-gods in different countries point to a common origin which is, of course, in the dark past, far beyond the sight of modern man. As the same god is often found in different countries and places under different names, it would take up too much space to attempt to list them all, and would serve no useful purpose. Various names of the same gods have been given when its fame has warranted it. Stories of the gods have been enriched and lengthened by the addition of the adventures of famous heroes who actually lived. In fact all the stories probably had their origin in the deeds of men renowned for their skill and courage.

CHAPTER **9**

Glossary of Smith Surnames

IN the following pages there has been collected and defined the many names in which Smith is either a suffix or a prefix, as well as the variations of the name. The same name is sometimes derived from two or more entirely different sources. As the name Smith is so common, it must be recognized that a variation or compound of the name may occur in more than one way, which is not unusual when studying the history of names. No history of a particular name can be accepted as final, however, without documentary evidence.

Because of space limitations, the author has not defined names such as Goldsmyth and Fieldsmyth where he has defined Goldsmith and Fieldsmith. The difference between the *y* and the *i* is explained in Chapter 1. Each name could doubtless be spelled in a great number of ways, but no useful purpose would be served by listing all of them here. The variations have been listed only when they were deemed important.

Every name in this chapter has been taken from some ancient list of names, city directory, book on names, newspaper, or through personal experience. Some of these forms are now undoubtedly obsolete. It was often possible to take a combination which, it was believed, would be taken by some as a surname, and then find it upon reference to a city directory or other large alphabetical list of names.

Dr. P. H. Reaney (*The Origin of English Surnames*, London, 1967) lists some names terminating in *-smith* that he says have been lost, but most of which have been observed by this writer. The Cushman made suich or thigh armor, and the word has been often corrupted into *kill* as evidenced by the rare surname, Kissman. Before he was married this author induced his intended to search in various directories for names terminating in *-smith*, and particularly for *Kissmith* but if it ever became a surname, it died out. Many of the names are translations from the German.

Various other combinations of smith are found as words or place names and were in existence at the time surnames were being taken, or soon after, which have not been found as surnames, although they may exist as such. Some examples are Boilersmith, Bertsmith, Brassmith, Chimneysmith, Framesmith, Garsmith, Gersmith, Helmsmith, Kersmith, Platinumsmith, Randsmith, Smithdown, Swordsmith, Treowsmith, and Weaponsmith. Webster's Dictionary lists thirty-nine of these words, many of which came into existence long after the surname period. They are grouped under the article headed -smith.

Thomas A. Edison has been called the Wondersmith of the World. Chopin has been described as a cunning fingersmith. The late Waldo Warren, who won considerable renown for coining the word "radio" to take the place of "wireless," has been dubbed a merchandising namesmith. Some newspapers have headed their joke section, "With the Funsmiths."

Humorous combinations of the word are found besides jokesmiths, puzzlesmith, songsmith and versesmith, such as adsmith, columnsmith, tunesmith and wordsmith. Many of these compounds as well as some of the above are found as hyphenated words. A newspaper comic strip includes a Dr. Errorsmith.

AIMSMITH—A corruption of Ainsmith, *q.v.* The letter *n* sometimes fades into *m*.

AINSMITH—In the Gaelic *ain,* a shortened form of *abhainn,* signifies a spring or river. This is a local name meaning the smith who lived by the river. The Gaelic *ain* also has a meaning of praiseworthy, respectful, honorable, and the name may have arisen from a title of respect thus given to some prominent smith in the community.

ALDERSMITH—The older smith, from the Early English *alder,* older. This name was probably first used to distinguish the parent or grand-parent from the younger smith. In Early English *alder* was used to denote the head of a family. It has also been suggested that it might be the smith who lived at the alder-tree, a tree related to the birch. See Youngsmith.

ALLINSMITH—Probably a combination of Allin and Smith.

ANCHORSMITH—The smith who made anchors. In his poem, *The Anchorsmiths,* Charles Dibdin writes,

"with forks the fire they goad,
And now twelve anchorsmiths the heaving bellows load;
While arm'd from every danger, and in grim array,
Anxious as howling demons waiting for their prey:
The forge the anchor yields from out its fiery maw,
Which, on the anvil prone, the cavern shouts harraw!

To save from adverse winds and waves the gallant British fleet."

ANKELSMITH—An early form of Anchorsmith, *q.v.*

ANKERSMITH—An early spelling of Anchorsmith, *q.v.*

ARASMITH—From the Gaelic *ara* meaning a tract of country; the name seems therefore to be a local name. In some English provincial dialects *aras* is a substantive plural of arrows, and in this case the name would be synonymous with Arrowsmith, *q.v.*

AREVESMYTH—An early form of Arrowsmith, *q.v.*

ARMSMITH—The smith who made armor and weapons, from the Gaelic *airm* meaning arms, weapons, or armor

AROUSMYTH—An early form of arrowsmith, *q.v*

AROWSMITH—Variant of Arrowsmith *q.v.*

ARRASMITH—If this name is from the Gaelic, it probably means the treacherous smith. It may, however be the same as Arasmith, *q.v.*

ARROSMITH—Variant of Arrowsmith, *q.v.*

ARROWESMITH—See Arrowsmith.

ARROWSMITH—Maker of arrows, especially arrowheads. In the days of archery this was an important and distinct trade. In 1405 a law was passed in England to compel the arrowsmiths to do better work. During the latter part of the eighteenth century and the first half of the nineteenth century this was the name of a famous English family of geographers. Martin Arrowsmith is the chief character in Sinclair Lewis's famous novel, *Arrowsmith*.

ARSMITH—A worker in brass from the Anglo-Saxon *ar,* brass. Some claim that it is a contraction of Arrowsmith, *q.v.*, but this seems to be clearly in error.

ARUESMYTH—An early form of Arrowsmith, *q.v.*

ARUSMYTH—An early form of Arrowsmith, *q.v.*

ARWESMYTH—An early spelling of Arrowsmith, *q.v.* This is the old English *arwe,* an arrow.

ATHERSMITH—The man "at ther smethe," or at the level field. Some contend that it is a corruption of Arrowsmith, *q.v.* It has also been claimed that it is a variant of the Anglo-Saxon *aethel,* noble, but this does not seem probable.

AXSMITH—The smith who made the old battle-ax, a weapon used in warfare in the fourteenth and fifteenth centuries.

BALISMITH—The bellow-smith, that is, a smith who uses a pair of bellows. From Old Norse *baelg,* boelig, meaning bag or bellows.

BALYSMYTH—A spelling of Balismith, *q.v.*

BARRETTSMITH—The smith who worked in the bright metals, from Old High German *beraht.*

BAUERNSMITH—A variant of Bauersmith, *q.v.*

BAUERSMITH—From the German *Bauerschmidt,* which means a country smith, the German word *bauer* meaning a peasant or countryman. The fact that one smith was from the country would often be used to distinguish him from another smith.

BAUSMITH—This name is from the German, where *bau* means building or working of a mine. The name would thus refer to the smith whose work related to the mine. In some cases it may be a contraction of Bauersmith, *q.v.*

BEILSMITH—From the German *Beilschmidt,* which means the smith who made hatchets or axes. The early bearers of this name probably made the battle-axe. The English form of the name would be Axsmith, *q.v.*

BELLSMITH—The smith who made bells. That the name is a translation of the German surnames of *Klingelschmidt* and *Schellenschmidt* does not seem probable, but it might be an explanation of the English name. It might also be a shortened form of Bellowsmith, or maker of smith's bellows.

BERINGSMITH—A combination of Bering and Smith, brought about by the intermarriage of the two families.

BEYLSMIT—One who made axes, a Dutch name.

BIERSMITH—From German *bier*, beer, designating the smith who brewed beer.

BILLSMITH—This is from the Anglo-Saxon *bill*, a word designating the warrior's battle-axe or sword, combined with *smith*, and indicates the smith who made them. In Middle English *bill* referred to a kind of pike or halberd, with a two-edged blade, carried by the English infantry. Later it became the usual weapon of watchmen. In Shakespeare, *Much Ado About Nothing*, III, 3, 44, is found the warning, "Have a care that your bills be not stoln." It is sometimes knows as a brownbill.

BLACKSMITH—A worker in iron, the black metal. Samuel Johnson, in his Dictionary, says that this smith is called this because he was very smutty. While the more general use of this term is modern, it is occasionally found in early writings, such as *Cocke Lorelles Bote*, (16th Cent.) so finding it as a surname is not surprising. But as the use of the term in early times is rare, the use of it as a surname is limited.

BLADESMITH—Maker of tools. Perhaps a sword manufacturer. The leaf-like, cutting part of an instrument, as distinguished from the handle, was made of metal by the smith, and since it was the most important part, the whole instrument was often called a blade.

BLADSMITH—Variant of Bladesmith, *q.v.*

BLAKESMYTH—An early spelling of Blacksmith, *q.v.* It has also been found as Blake-Smythe.

BLECKSMITH—This is an Anglicized form of the German *Blechschmidt*, meaning tinsmith, or worker in tin.

BOKELSMYTH—An early spelling of Bucklesmith, *q.v.*

BOCKSMITH—The smith by the beech tree, from Old English *boc* beech tree; or the schmidt by the brook from German *bach* brook.

BOLTSMITH—A maker of bolts, or arrows, from Old English *bolt*, a heavy short arrow with blunt head to be shot from the crossbow or other engine of war.

BOTSMITH—The smith who made metal fittings on boats, or perhaps a boat-building, from Old English *bat* meaning boat.

BOWERSMITH—A variant of Boyersmith, *q.v.*

BOWSMITH—The smith who made the bows. In early times bows were generally made of wood but later they were often made of steel, especially the strong crossbows, and thus came to be manufactured by the smiths.

BOYERSMITH—The smith who made bows, from the English *bowyer.* See Bowsmith.

BRESSELSMITH—The schmidt who came from Breslau, a city in Germany.

BROCKSMITH—The smith who lived or worked by the brook, from Middle English *brock,* brook, spelled broc and *brok.*

BROEKSMIT—The smith who lived near the brook.

BROOKSMITH—The smith who lived or worked by the brook. See Brocksmith for early spelling.

BROSMITH—This is probably a contraction of brord-smith, and designates the smith who made the *broard,* an Anglo-Saxon word meaning a lance or javelin.

BROUNESMYTH—An early spelling of Brownsmith, *q.v.*

BROUNSMYTH—An early form of Brownsmith, *q.v.*

BROWNSMITH—Signifies the smith who did the bright or burnished work and is opposite to blacksmith. Also defined as one who worked in copper and brass. In some cases it may refer to the smith who made the brownbills, a two-edged sickle-shaped knife or sword, weighing from nine to twelve pounds, on a handle three or four feet long, and wielded with both hands with terrible power. In a few cases it refers to the smith with brown hair or complexion.

BUCKLESMITH—One who made buckles. "Bokell-smythes" are mentioned in *Cocke Lorelle's Bote* (16th Cent.).

BUCKSMITH—Contraction of Bucklesmith, *q.v.*

BURSMITH—The farmer smith, from Old Low German *bur.*

CALDERSMITH—The smith who lived by the Calder, the name of several rivers in England.

CAMBESMITH—The smith who made combs of iron (used in dressing wool, flax, etc.)

CARLSMITH—A coalescing of the forename *Carl* and the surname *Smith.* At least this is the case in two known instances. The Germanic *carl* originally denoted a man or male person. In the

Scandinavian countries it acquired the meaning of "strong man," and this might well have been used with smith as a description.

CHAPPELSMITH—The smith who lived or worked near the chapel. This may, however, refer to the Middle English *chape,* that is, the metal plate or mounting of a sheath, and thus designate the smith who made them.

CHARLESSMITH—A coalescing of the forename *Charles* to the surname *Smith.*

CHAROONSMITH—Probably a combination of *Charoon* and *Smith.*

CHEMITT—Form of the German *Schmidt* found among the Creoles in Louisiana.

CHIETESMYTH—The smith who cuts, from the Anglo-Norman *chete,* meaning to cut. It might also refer to the forest smith, from British *ceto.*

CHITELSMYTH—From Old English *cietel,* kettle, the smith who made kettles.

CHMID—Form of the German Schmid found among the Creoles in Louisiana.

CLARKSMITH—The clergyman or scribe who did smith work.

CLAYSMITH—The smith who lived at the clayey place.

CLEINESMITH—This is an Anglicized form of the German *Kleinschmidt,* the smith who made small objects, or in some cases, the small smith. In English since the Norman Conquest, due to the influence of the French, the letter *c* has taken the place of the *k* in many instances, particularly when it precedes an *l.*

CLINGINGSMITH—A corruption of Klingensmith, *q.v.*

CLOCKSMITH—The smith who made clocks.

COKESMYTH—The smith who was a cook, from the Old English spelling *coke.* The name occurs in the Boldon Book, and there undoubtedly designated one who was a cook as well as a smith.

COLSMITH—The smith who used coal, from anglo-Saxon *col,* in contrast with the smith who used wood. Or it may refer to the smith who worked cold—without fire.

COOPERSMITH—The smith who made tubs, casks, etc. But at least one authority thinks that it is a wrong translation of the German *Kupferschmied,* i.e. coppersmith. It might, however, be a mere variation of the English Coppersmith, *q v.*

COPERSMITH—Man early spelling of Coppersmith, *q.v.*

COPPERSMITH—One who works in copper. The coppersmith also worked with brass. Paul, in his second letter to Timothy (II Timothy iv, 14) says, "Alexander, the coppersmith did me much evil."

CROSSMITH—The smith by the cross. It might, however, have the occupation meaning of the cross-bow maker. It might also be a variant of Grossmith.

CROWLESMITH—The smith who dwelt by the crow-lea, the meadow infested by crows.

DEGELSMITH—The secret or hidden smith, from Old English *degle,* meaning secret or hidden. One authority, however, suggests that it is from *degen,* an old cant term for sword or dagger.

DeSMITH—De is usually prefixed properly only to place names, and, if this is not merely an affectation, it designates the person who came from a place called Smith.

DIRSMITH—The smith who made doors and locks for doors.

D'SMITH—A variant of De Smith, *q.v.*

EBBSMITH—Possibly the smith who lived by the Ebble River, a small stream in Wiltshire, England, from Old English *ebba,* low tide. After Arthur W. Pinero staged his play *The Notorious Mrs. Ebbsmith,* a lady with that surname committed suicide.

EDSCHMID—The schmidt by the wasteland or uncultivated field.

EISENSMITH—From the German *Eisenschmidt,* which might be translated ironsmith. The name no doubt originated to distinguish the worker in iron from the smith who dealt with some other metal.

ELSMITH—The foreign smith, from the Anglo-Saxon prefix *El*— meaning strange or foreign. Many skillful smiths from other countries were often imported by the knights, or brought back with them after the wars.

ENGLESMITH—The smith who came from England; the smith on the meadow or grassland.

ERROLSMYTHE—From the German *Erle,* the alder-tree, and refers to the smith who worked nearby.

ESMITE—A Spanish or Mexican form of Smith.

ESMITH—The E- prefix is an archaic dialectal form of the Anglo-Saxon prefix *ze-,* now practically obsolete except in the archaic

form *y-*, found in such words as Yclept, ybent, etc. It is cognate with the German *ge-*. Although this prefix is sometimes found added to many words, it is usually found in connection with verbs, and it is likely that this name is from a verb. In some cases the general sense of the simple verb is limited by the prefix, while in others no difference in meaning is discernable, as seems to be true in the present instance.

EXSMICHT—A Scottish early form of Exsmyth. See Axsmith.

EXSMYTH—A form of Axsmith, *q.v.*

FAURESMITH—The French *Faure* is a rather common name meaning the worker in iron, and thus is synonymous with the English *smith*. As a surname the compound probably arose from a smith who, having earned the name or description Faure in France, came to England and plied his trade. To an acquired surname of Faure the English might have added smith as an explanatory or, to them, descriptive word.

FEINSMITH—One who made fine delicate objects or ornamentation.

FEWSMITH—The fewster, or smith who made the wooden framework of the saddle-tree.

FIELDSMITH—The smith who sharpened the picks of miners. A mine is called by the pitman a field. The German *feldschmiede* means forge of an army blacksmith, and the name *Fieldsmith* may thus indicate an army blacksmith.

FINESMITH—The smith who was a refiner of gold or silver, from Anglo-Saxon *fineur,* a goldsmith.

FINSMITH—Variant of Feinsmith or Finesmith, *q.v.*

FITZSMITH—The son of the smith, from the Anglo-Norman *fiz* (pronounced fitz).

FOLKSMITH—An obsolete meaning of folk is retainers or servants, and the surname here means the servant of the smith. It may, however, be a coalescing of Fulk and the surname Smith, or it may mean "the son of Fulk Smith." Fulk was once a popular Christian name; it is an old English name, of Teutonic origin, meaning people's guard.

FORDSMITH—The smith by the river crossing.

FORESMITH—The smith in the front or fore, from old English *fore.*

FORSMITH—Variant of Foresmith, *q.v.*

FOSTERSMITH—The forester-smith, the smith who lived or worked in the forest.

FREISMITH—The Anglicized form of the German *Freischmidt,* literally free smith, indicating the smith who was free, or not a member of the guild.

FREUSMITH—A corruption of Freismith, *q.v.*

GALESMITH—The smith who made gales, the crane over a grate.

GARNERSMITH—The smith who lived by the granary or storehouse, from Middle English *garner.*

GASSENSMITH—The German word *gassen* means a street or lane, and the early bearer of this name probably lived and had his shop on *the* street.

GAUDSMITH—The smith who worked or lived in the forest; sometimes a coalescing of the French forename *Gaud* and the surname *Smith.*

GILDSMITH—One who gilds, a gilder, from Old English *gyldan.* Also a spelling of Goldsmith, *q.v.*

GOADSMITH—Variant of Goodsmith, *q.v.*

GODESMITH—An ancient spelling of Goodsmith, *q.v.*

GOLDESMYTH—An archaic spelling of Goldsmith, *q.v.*

GOLDSMITH—A worker, or seller, of gold articles; a jeweler; a banker. The goldsmith also handled silver articles, and really included the trade of the silversmith too, hence the relative frequency of the name Goldsmith as compared with Silversmith. The medieval goldsmiths, or workers in gold, were persons of consequence. They entered the profitable business of banking as they were the only ones in the community who had safe places in which to store things of great value. They loaned vast sums to the government of England and in 1672 when Charles II closed the Exchequer and suspended payment they were creditors of the treasury to the sum of L1,300,000. They became insolvent and the Bank of England succeeded them in 1694. They were later paid (1706). Three tenants-in-chief under the Conqueror are entered in Domesday Book under the name of Aurifaber. The equivalent French *Orfevre* and the German *Goldschmidt* are well-known surnames. The most famous man with this name was Oliver Goldsmith (1728-1774), the Irish author. A goldsmithess was a female goldsmith.

GOLDSMYTH—An early form of Goldsmith, *q.v.*

GOLDSMITHE—An early form of Goldsmith, *q.v.*

GOODSMITH—From the nickname, "the good smith," which probably refers to his ability at the forge rather than to his moral character.

GORDONSMITH—The smith by the gore-hill, or three-cornered hill, from Old English *gara*, plus *dun*, a hill.

GOUDSMIT—A Dutch form of Goldsmith, *q.v.*

GOULDSMITH—An early variation of Goldsmith, *q.v.*

GRANTSMITH—The big smith, from French *grand*.

GREENESMITH—An old spelling of Greensmith, *q.v.*

GREENSMITH—The smith who worked in lead. Some have suggested that this name refers to the smith who lived at the green, and this is undoubtedly the explanation in some cases.

GRENSMITH—Variant of Greensmith, *q.v.*

GREYSMITH—Probably refers to the smith with the gray hair. It may designate the reeve, i.e. bailiff or steward, from the Anglo-Saxon *gerefa*, who was a smith. Another possible origin is that it denotes the smith who lived by the grove, from the Anglo-Saxon *graf*. The first meaning seems preferable.

GRIMESMITH—The smith who made the *grima*, an Anglo-Saxon word meaning mask, visor, helmet. It might also be the cruel, grim, savage smith, from the Anglo-Saxon *grim* with that meaning.

GROSSMITH—This is the English form of the German *Grossschmidt* which means a maker of heavy iron articles, being opposite to the *Kleinschmidt*, i.e. small smith or maker of locks. It also has a meaning of big smith. It might be adapted from the German *Grobschmied*, blacksmith. Weedon Grossmith (1853-1919) was a well-known English comedian.

GUNSMITH—The smith who made guns. It is not surprising to find this as a name when it is remembered that firearms were used in European warfare as early as the 14th century and came into practical use in the next century.

HACKENSMITH—The English form of the German *Hackenschmidt*, which refers to the smith who made hoes.

HAMMERSMITH—One who came from Hammersmith, now a part of London, England, originally Hammerschmiede, literally Saxon for blacksmith's shop. In its early history this village had a great number of smithies. The New English Dictionary defines

hammersmith as a smith who works with a hammer but this does not sound convincing since practically all smiths worked with a hammer.

HAMSMITH—A contraction of Hammersmith, *q.v.* It may indicate the smith at the level pasture or river-meadow, from the Old English *ham.*

HARRISMITH—Variant of Harrowsmith, *q.v.* In Scotland and Yorkshire, England, a harrow was called a harry.

HARROWSMITH—The same as Arrowsmith, *q.v.,* being the aspirate form.

HAVERSMITH—From Middle English *haver,* oats, and referred to a smith who lived near an oatfield.

HEITSMITH—The English form of the German Heitsmidt, referring to the smith who lived by the heath, the open uncultivated land.

HIGHSMITH—Nicknamed "the high smith," meaning the tall or distinguished looking smith. The Old English *high* also means great, illustrious, noble, and an important smith in the community may have been so designated.

HILDSMITH—The smith who made sword hilts. It might, however, be connected with the Anglo-Saxon *hild,* meaning battle

or war, and thus designate a soldier. Hyldsmyth is found in the Hundred Rolls of 1273.

HILLSMITH—This seems to be the same as Hildsmith, *q.v.* It is possible, however, that it means the smith who lived on or near a hill, but the above seems preferable, for if the latter meaning were correct, it would probably be Smithhill.

HINDESMITH—The smith who was a servant, from the Middle English *hine,* a peasant or servant. This name is sometimes seen as a misspeing for the surname of Paul Hindemith, the German composer.

HOCKENSMITH—From the German *Hackenschmidt,* the smith who made hoes or hatchets. The German word *hocken* means to squat. If the name is English, it means the "son of Henry Smith," from the nickname Hal, diminutive Halkin, often written Hawkin and corrupted to Hockin.

HOCKERSMITH—The smith with the hunchback, from the German *hocker* with that meaning.

HOOPERSMITH—The smith who made iron hoops for barrels, casks, tubs, etc. Compare with the first meaning given under Coopersmith.

HUDSMITH—The smith who made hoods or helmets, from old English *hod,* hood.

HUFFSMITH—From the German *Huffschmidt,* the maker of horseshoes. The practice of shoeing horses is said to have been carried from the Continent to England by William the Conqueror.

HUFSMITH—From the German *Hufschmidt.* See Huffsmith.

HYLDSMYTH—Variant of Hildsmith, *q.v.*

HYSMITH—Variant of Highsmith, *q.v.*

JAYSMITH—This was originally John Smith, written J. Smith and changed to John Jaysmith for the sake of distinction.

JOYSMITH—Probably Joy, the smith.

KALSMITH—The cold smith, the brazier who worked without fire.

KEMPSMITH—The smith who did work for the soldiers, from Middle English *kemp,* a warrior.

KENTSMITH—The smith who came from Kent, the county in England.

KINGSMITH—The king's smith.

KIRSMITH—The smith who lived or had his forge near the church.

KLAYSMITH—From the German *Klaischmidt.* See Claysmith.

KLEINSMITH—English form of the German *Kleinschmidt,* meaning small smith, used with reference to the product of the smith's work, distinguishing the smith who made small objects such as nails, locks, keys, etc., from the constructor of the large grilles and doors. In some cases it described the smith's stature.

KLINESMITH—Variant of Kleinsmith, *q.v.*

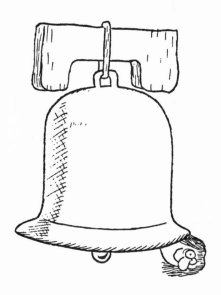

KLINGELSMITH—The English form of the German Klingelschmidt, the smith who made bells.

KLINGENSMITH—From the German *Klingenschmidt,* the smith who made blades, the name being equivalent to the English Bladesmith, *q.v.*

KLINGERSMITH—The smith who made bells, from the German *klingel,* bell. It might also refer to an especially noisy German smith.

KLINGINSMITH—Variant of Klingensmith, *q.v.*

KLINGLESMITH—The smith who made bells. From the German *klingel,* bell.

KNIFESMITH—The smith who made knives, a cutler. The word *knife* was also used in the past to include a sword. In the Anglo-Saxon the usual word for knife was *seax,* which meant a small sword or dagger. Thus the knifesmith was a swordsmith.

KNIVESMITH—An early spelling of Knifesmith, *q.v.*

KNYFESMYTHE—Variant of Knifesmith, *q.v.*

KNYFSMITH—Variant of Knifesmith, *q.v.*

KNYSMITH—See Knifesmith. This is an early spelling.

KOOPERSMITH—Variant of Coopersmith, *q.v.*

KOPERSMITH—Variant of Coppersmith, *q.v.*

KOPPERSMITH—The English form of the German *Kopperschmidt*, which means coppersmith. See Coppersmith.

KUPERSMITH—From the German *Kupperschmidt*, i.e. Coppersmith, *q.v.*

KUPFERSMITH—From the German *Kupferschmidt*, meaning coppersmith.

KUPPERSMITH—The worker in copper, from the German Kupperschmidt.

LANGSMITH—An English and Scottish form of Longsmith, *q.v.*

LANGGESMYTH—An early spelling of Longsmith, *q.v.*

LEDSMYTH—The smith who worked in lead, from Old English *lead*.

LEESMITH—This name may be an arbitrary invention or combination of two other names as the only instance found is that of J. S. Smith of Slingsby, York, who, in 1879, changed his name to Leesmith. Lee is a modification of the Anglo-Saxon *leah*, which corresponds to the English *lea* signifying a meadow, pasture or grass land. The name might thus designate a smith who lived by the meadow or grass land if it is not an arbitrary combination.

LEYSMYTH—One who worked in *lay*, a pewterer.

LINDENSMITH—A translation of the German *Lindenschmidt*. The name refers to the smith who lived by or near the linden tree. Battle shields were often made of linden wood, and this in some cases might be the smith who made them.

LINDESMITH—Variant of Lindensmith, *q.v.*

LITTELSMYTH—The small or short smith. An early spelling.

LOCKSMITH—From the occupation, locksmith. It is interesting to note that as a surname the occupation has taken the form Lockyer, while locksmith has become the usual occupation term.

LOCSMYTH—A form of Locksmith, *q.v.*

LOKERSMYTH—From Old English *locer*, plane, and thus this refers to the smith who made planes.

LOKSMYTHE—An old variation of Locksmith, *q.v.*

LONGSMITH—From the nickname, "the long smith," which referred to the smith's tall stature.

LOXSMYTH—A spelling of Locksmith, *q.v.*

LYDESMYTH—The smith who worked in lead.

McSMITH—The son of the smith.

MANNASMITH—The man who lived near the smithy (the smith's place), from the Celtic or Cymric *man* or *maen,* a place or district, an element often found in place names. Variant of Mannersmith, *q.v.*

MANNERSMITH—The smith in the manor or village.

MANSMITH—Variant of Mannasmith, *q.v.*

MARKSMITH—The smith who lived by the boundary.

MARTINSMITH—Probably Martin, the smith.

MAYOSMITH—A conbination of Mayo, a corrupt form of Matthew and the surname Smith. The name probably arose in an attempt to differentiate one surname of Smith from another, since it was necessary to use the father's full name as a surname rather than just his surname of Smith. A connection with County Mayo in Ireland does not seem likely.

MESSERSMITH—From the German *Messerschmidt,* denoting the smith who made knives.

MEYERSMITH—The origin of this name is similar to that of Smithmeyer, *q.v.*, although in some cases it may be a combination of two surnames.

MINSMITH—One who forged the coin, at the mint smithy, a minter.

MONASMITH—A variant of Monesmith, *q.v.*

MONESMITH—The smith who made money. Same as the Mintsmith or Minsmith, *q.v.*

MONEYSMITH—Variant of Monesmith, *q.v.*

MONOSMITH—Variant of Monesmith, *q.v.*

MYMERSMYTH—A nickname given to an excellent and skilled smith in reference to the legendary smith, Mimer, who was slain by the sword, Grauer, wielded by Sigurd.

MYNSMITH—Variant of Minsmith, *q.v.*

NAESMYTH—Same as Nasmyth, *q.v.*
  The family of Naesmyth of Posso, in the county of Peebles, are said to derive their name from the following circumstances:— During the reign of Alexander III of Scotland, the ancestor of the family was, on the eve of a battle, required by him to repair his armor. Although a man of great stature and power, he was unsuccessful. After the battle, having performed feats of valour, he was knighted by the king, who remarked, "although he was *nae smith,* he was a brave gentleman."

  A similar legend, dear to every Naesmith, but probably an etiological myth, has it that their ancestor was 'nae smith at al,' but a canny Scotchman who was a staunch supporter of his king in the feuds between him and his powerful subjects. So 'ye Antient Chronicall of Naesmyth' tells of an encounter in which the king's men, beaten by the Douglas faction, sought safety through retreat. One entered a smith's shop, hastily donned an apron, seized a hammer and was busily helping the smith when the pursuers arrived. In his excitement he delivered a blow so unskillfully that the shaft of the hammer broke upon the anvil. This betrayed him and one of the Douglas party rushed at him exclaiming, "Ye're nae smyth at all." The assailed man seized his sword, lying concealed near by, and killed his assailant, while the real smith brained another of the party with his hammer. Unfortunately, some of the king's men who had rallied now happened along and overpowered them all. Later, so the story runs, the king bestowed a grant of land upon his royal henchman and gave him the surname *Naesmith.*

NAGELSMITH—From the German *Nagelschmidt,* a nailer; same as the English Nailsmith, *q.v.*

NAILSMITH—The smith who made spikes and nails.

NAISMITH—Nail maker. Same as Nailsmith, *q.v.* But see also Naesmyth and Nasmyth. James Naismith invented the game of basketball, in 1891, in Plainfield, Mass.

NASMYTH—A nailsmith or nail-maker. It has also been suggested that this might be derived from Knifesmith, but the evidence for this theory is slight.

NAYSMITH—Variant of Naismith, *q.v.*

NEASMITH—Variant of Nailsmith, *q.v.* Some claim that this is the same as Knifesmith.

NEGGESMITH—The smith at the corner, from Gaelic *N-uig,* sometimes found, as a place name, in the form *Nigg.* It could be the smith who made nails, from Old English naegel.

NESMITH—Variant of Neasmith, *q.v.* It is sometimes found as Ne-smith and Ne Smith.

NEWLANDSMITH—This seems to be the running together of a hyphenated name as it is found also as Newland-Smith.

NICKLESMITH—The dwarf or demon smith, from the German *nickel* meaning dwarf, rascal, mischievous demon. At the time when surnames were being adopted, nickel was not used much. The Germans applied the term *kupfernickel* to the mineral because, despite its copper-colored appearance, it actually yielded no copper.

NOELSMITH—A coalescing of the Christian name *Noel* (Christmas) with the surname *Smith.*

OAKESMITH—See Oaksmith.

OAKSMITH—Probably designated the smith at the oak; the smith who had his forge under an oak tree.

OLDSMITH—The old smith, so called to differentiate him from the young smith. Cf. Aldersmith.

ORRINSMITH—A coalescing of the Christian name *Orrin* (white of skin) with the surname *Smith*.

ORSMYTH—A smith who works in ore (here probably copper or brass). See Arsmith.

OVERSMITH—The smith at the shore or river-bank, from Old English *ōfer*.

OWENSMITH—Probably a coalescing of *Owen* and *Smith*.

PANSMITH—The smith who made pans.

PINSMITH—From the old English *pinn*, a peg or pin. It designated the maker of pins, small needles and other wire articles.

PITTSMITH—The smith at the pit, from Old English *pyt*.

PLATESMITH—One who hammered the metal into plates, or flat dishes. Armor plates were made for the armorer who then fashioned them into armor.

PLOUSMITH—Variant of Plowsmith, *q.v.*

PLOWSMITH—The smith who made plows.

POTTSMITH—The smith who made pots, from Old English *pott*.

REDESMITH—A worker in gold, or goldsmith, from the color of the metal. It also designated the smith who had red hair.

REINSMITH—Variation of Rheinsmith, *q.v.*

RHEINSMITH—From the German Rheinschmidt, meaning the smith who lived by the river Rhine.

RHINESMITH—A more fully Anglicized form of Rheinschmidt than Reinsmith, *q.v.*

RINESMITH—An Anglicized form of the German Rheinschmidt. See Rheinsmith.

RINGSMITH—As a prefix, *ring* is from Old English *hring* and means chain armor and it would be natural to call the smith who made that armor a Ringsmith. The word also refers to any circular metal.

RIVERSMITH—The smith who lived or worked by the river.

RODESMITH—A variation of Redesmith, *q.v.* It might have designated the smith at the clearing, or open space in the forest, from the Middle English *rode*. In some cases, it might also have indicated the smith who lived by the road. It has been suggested that he might be the manufacturer of the then familiar "rood" or "rode," the cross which we occasionally still see standing beside the old English turnpikes.

RODSMITH—Variant of Rodesmith, *q.v.*

ROKESMITH—The smith who lived at the rock, from Old French *roke.*

SAXSMYTH—Same as Sixsmith, *q.v.*

SCASMITH—Variant of Scythesmith, *q.v.*

SCHEIRSMYTH—An early Scottish form of Shearsmith, *a.v.*

SCHELLSMITH—A partially Anglicized form of the German *Schellenschmidt,* meaning the smith who made bells.

SCHERSMYTH—An early form of Shearsmith, *q.v.*

SCHMIDT, SCHMID, SCHMIT, SCHMITT, SCHMIED—German forms of Smith.

SCHMITH—A partially Anglicized form of the German *Schmidt.* Compare with Shmith.

SCHMITHER—See Schmith and Smither.

SCHMITT—A German form of Smith.

SCHMITTSCHMITT—See explanation in Chapter 6.

SCHMITZ—The patronymic genitive form of the German *Schmidt.*

SCHMITZER—The German Schmitz with the analogical suffix *er* added.

SCMITT—A variation of the German *Schmitt,* the *h* having dropped out.

SCOTTSMITH—This is from Old English *scot,* a dart or small javelin, and designates the smith who made them. It may also mean a smith who came from Scotland.

SCYTHESMITH—One who made scythes, especially the old weapon known by that term in the-thirteenth to sixteenth centuries, having a long curving blade resembling a reaping hook. As an agricultural implement it is mentioned as early as the eighth century A.D.

SERSMITH—Variant of Shearsmith, *q.v.*

SEVERSMITH—The maker of sieves, from the old English *sife.* May also be the wire smith, from Old English *siever,* a wiremaker. *Siever* is also a pet form of Siegfried, and the name thus may be a coalescing of *Siever* and the surname *Smith.*

SEXSMITH—Same as Sixsmitn, *q.v.*

SHARESMITH—The smith who made shares, the iron blade in a plough which cuts the ground, now better known as a ploughshare. Reference to the share is found in *Corpus Glosses* c. 725, there spelled *scaer*. The German *Schaarschmidt* is cognate with this name, and as a surname it may have been translated from the German in some instances.

SHARSMITH—A variant of Sharesmith, *q.v.*

SHAWSMITH—The smith beside the shaw, a small wood or grove.

SHEARSMITH—This name may have the same meaning as Brownsmith, *q.v.*, from Anglo-Saxon *scit,* bright, but it is more likely the same as the German *Schaarschmidt.* Anglo-Saxon *scer* means ploughshare. It may also be a maker of shears, perhaps similar to the bladesmith.

SHEERSMITH—An Anglicized form of the German *Scheerschmidt* meaning the smith who made shears. In some cases it may be a variation of Shearsmith, *q.v.* It has also been defined as one who shears sheep, but this last theory is unlikely.

SHERESMYTH—An early spelling of Sheersmith, *q.v.*

SHEWSMITH—Variant of Shoesmith, *q.v.*

SHMIT—Same as the German *Schmit.* Here the name has been changed one letter towards the English form.

SHMITH—Same as Smith; Englished from the German *Schmidt.*

SHOESMITH—From the occupation, shoesmith, a maker of horseshoes, a farrier. Today the word is obsolete, but it was quite common until the last century. There are various forms of this name due to the many early spellings of shoe. Farriers and shoesmiths gradually exceeded their function and took care of the health of horses, thus becoming the forerunners of veternarians.

SHOOSMITH—Variant of shoesmith, *q.v.* The Middle English spelling of shoe was often *shoo.*

SHOOWSMYTH—Variant of Shoosmith. See Shoesmith.

SHOSMITH—An early spelling of Shoesmith, *q.v.*

SHUCKSMITH—Variant of Shoesmith, *q.v.*, from an early German dialectal spelling of shoe.

SHUESMITH—Same as Shoesmith, *q.v.*, from an early spelling.

SHUGHSMITH—Variant of Shoesmith, *q.v.*

SHUGSMYTH—A variation of Shughsmith. See Shoesmith.

SHUKESMITH—Variant of Shoesmith, *q.v.*

SHUSMITH—Variant of Shoesmith, *q.v.*, from a Middle English spelling.

SHUXSMITH—Variant of Shoesmith, *q.v.*

SICKELSMITH—From the German *Sichelschmidt,* which is the same as Sicklesmith, *q.v.*

SICKLESMITH—The smith who made sickles, a crescent-shaped, agricultural implement similar to a reaping-hook except that it is provided with a serrated cutting-edge. It was common in England as early as the tenth century.

SICKSMITH—Same as Sixmith, *q.v.* It may, however, refer to the smith by the small stream, from Old English *sic.*

SICSMITH—This refers to the smith by the brook, from Old English *sic,* small stream.

SILVERSMITH—From the occupation, silversmith, in the same manner as goldsmith. But it is not nearly as common because the goldsmith generally included the work of the silversmith. See Goldsmith. In the Bible, "Demetrius, a silversmith," is mentioned in *Acts* xix, 24.

SISEMITH—See Sixsmith and Scythesmith. However, this is probably a variant of the latter.

SITHESMITH—Variant of Scythesmith, *q.v.*

SIXSMITH—The smith who made swords, from the Anglo-Saxon *seax,* sometimes found as *sex,* meaning a small sword or dagger. Some have suggested that this is a contraction of Sicklesmith, *q.v.*—but the first explanation seems more likely.

SKELYSMITH—A corruption of Sicklesmith, *q.v.*

SMEATH—Dweller on the smooth or level place, from the Anglo-Sax n *smaeth,* meaning smooth or even. The name often developed into Smith.

SMEATHERS—A corrupt form of Smithers, *q.v.*

SMEATHMAN—Probably a variant of Smitheman, *q.v.* A second meaning is the man by the smeath or smooth, level field.

SMEATON—The smooth or flat enclosure. Also has a meaning of the Smith's or Smiths' place.

SMEAYTH—An early Scottish form of Smith.

SMEDICK—One who came from Smethwick, *q.v.*

SMEE—Probably a reduction of Smeeth, *q.v.* It also means small. In Norfolk, *smeath,* signifying an open level of considerable extent, is pronounced *smee,* and thus would be the surname of one who lived near there.

SMEED—See Smeeth.

SMEETH—Local of Smeeth, a parish in Kent County, England. Also at the Smethe, a smooth place, from Anglo-Saxon *smaeth*. In the Devon dialect Smeeth is just a variation of Smith, as the *ee* was the equivalent of the letter *i*.

SMEETON—Variant of Smeaton, *q.v.*

SMEITH—An old spelling of Smith.

SMEITHTONE, SMEYTHTONE—Old Scottish forms of Smithton, *q.v.*

SMEITON—An Old Scottish form of Smeaton, *q.v.*

SMETH—Variant of Smeath, *q.v.* It is also found as a spelling of

SMEITHTONE, SMEYTHTONE—Old Scottish forms of Smithton, *q.v.*

SMEITON—An Old Scottish form of Smeaton, *q.v.*

SMETH—Variant of Smeath, *q.v.* It is also found as a spelling of Smith in the fourteenth and fifteenth centuries.

SMEATH—Dweller on the smooth or level place, from the Anglo-Saxon *smaeth,* meaning smooth or even. The name often developed into Smith.

SMETHEM—Variant of Smethan, *q.v.*

SMETHISSONE—A Scottish variant of Smithson, *q.v.*

SMETHURST—One who came from Smethurst, Lancaster County, England. Also designates a dweller at the smith's wood. See Smithurst.

SMETHWICK—Variant of Smithwick, *q.v.*

SMETON—A Scottish form of Smith. In a few cases a contraction of Smithton, *q.v.*

SMETTOUN—A Scottish form of Smeaton, *q.v.*

SMEY—In some cases this name may be a colloquial pronunciation of Smeth or Smith, but in most cases it is probably just a form of *smeath,* meaning a smooth, level field. In Norfolk *smeath* is pronounced *smee.*

SMEYTONE—An old Scottish form of Smithton, *q.v.*

SMEYTH—Variant of Smeith, *q.v.*

SMICHT—Scottish form of Smith.

SMID—A Saxon form of Smith. In early manuscripts we occasionally find *d* in places where we should have expected *th,* though the pronunciation is the same as *th.* The ð developed from the Anglo-Saxon letter *ot,* which took the place of our modern *th.*

The Old High German *smid* means a worker in metal. Many other languages have words from a radical *smi*, meaning to work in metal, to forge.

SMIDA—One who smiths, from the Old Norse verb *smiðta*, Old Frisian *Smitha*.

SMIDDIE—A Scottish variant of Smithy. See also Smiddy.

SMIDDY—One who worked in the smithy, from Old English *smiththe* or *smiððy*, the workshop of a smith.

SMIDH—Danish form of smith.

SMIDL—The little smith.

SMIDO, SMITHY, SMYTHIA—Baptismal names. Smith is generally a surname, but here we seem to have the three endings, *a*, *i*, (*y*) and *o*, the three characteristics of baptismal names.

SMIDT—A Low German form of smith.

SMIDTH—This name may have been derived from an old Anglo-Saxon spelling of smithy, *smiðtðte*. The first ð changed into *d* which is not unusual, while the second ð took its English equivalent *th*. Another explanation of this name is that it is a partially Anglicized, Low German form of Smith. It is also found as a Norwegian form. In the Lansdowne manuscript of Chaucer's *Canterbury Tales* (*Miller's Tale*, line 3761) smith is spelled smyththe (smyþþe).

SMIGH—A spelling of Smith. The Anglo-Saxon *g* was often substituted for *h*, and in time was written *gh*. The name probably arose from a local, irregular pronunciation of Smith. It may also be a variation of the Middle English *smeigh* meaning clever, cunning, skillful.

SMIGTH—A modernized spelling of Smyght, *q.v.* See also Smigh.

SMIJTH—A variation in spelling of Smith. (See Chapter 3)

SMIJTT—Variant of Smijth, *q.v.*

SMIRTHWAITE—Local of Smurthwaite, *q.v.*

SMISBY—One who came from Smisby, in Derbyshire. The place-name was earlier written Smithesby, the smith's place.

SMISSMAN—Variant of Smithman, *q.v.*

SMIT—A Low German form of Smith.

SMITTEEE—This is a curious Low German form of smith. The unusual ending of the name as far as the third *e* is concerned doubtlessly arose from mere caprice, probably after a phonetic spelling of the name, with a wish of the bearer to be different. Smitty is a common nickname of one named Smith, and this seems to be an instance where the nickname was adopted as the surname, with a variation in spelling.

SMITGEN—The little smith, from the German diminutive termination -chen.

SMITH—See Chapter 2.

SMITHA—In Anglo-Saxon names the a was a common ending, and its addition to a word implied connection with it. Thus Smitha designates one who is connected with a smith or smithy by adding an a to the root. Old Frisian smitha, a smithy, may have influenced the name. See Smithy.

SMITHAFER—The smith who lived near the shore, bank or border, from Old English ofer.

SMITHAM—Dweller at the smith's enclosure, or homestead, from the Anglo-Saxon ham, with that meaning. Ham is a common component syllable of many English surnames and place-names. Also one who worked with smitham, i.e. ore small enough to pass through the wire bottom of the sieve.

SMITHAN—The Old English -an was a genitive singular ending, often added to a personal name. The -an was often corrupted into -ing. This may be from Old English han, a stone or rock and thus distinguished the smith who worked nearby.

SMITHANA—The smith who lived alone, from the Anglo-Saxon ana, meaning single, sole, solitary.

SMITHANDERS—This is the same as Smithman, derived from Swedish ander, meaning man.

SMITHANIUK—This is the Slavic smetana meaning sour cream, with the patronymical suffix uk, and thus means "son of Smetana," the surname Smetaniuk being Americanized under the influence of Smith.

SMITHARAN—Variant of Smitheran, q.v.

SMITHARD—The smith who lived by the ard, a Gaelic term meaning the height, or the hill.

SMITHART—The smith who was also the keeper or tender of a flock, from Old English heord.

SMITHAUSLER—The smith who was a cottager, that is, owner of a cottage with little land around it; from German hausler.

SMITHAVITCH—A variant of Smithevich, *q.v.*

SMITHBACK—An Anglicized form of the Norwegian farm name, Smetbak, a name of medium, or possibly low, rank in Norway.

SMITHBAIRD—Variant of Smythberd, *q.v.*

SMITHBAKER—This name doubtlessly arose from the fact that its original bearer, after earning the name Baker, or one whose father was a baker, became a smith.

SMITHBAUER—From the German *Schmidtbauer,* which designated a smith who came from the country. See Bauersmith.

SMITHBECK—One who lived or worked near the smith's brook, from Old English *beck,* a brook.

SMITHBERG—The smith who lived by the berg, that is, hill, from the Old High German *berg. Berg* was an early English form, which is now obsolete, of the word barrow, meaning a hill or hillock. The Anglo-Saxon *berg* also means a hill or mountain.

SMITHBERGER—A peasant smith or one who lived in the forest from the now obsolete *bergier* which may be defined as a peasant, a woodman.

SMITHBEY—The smith's homestead farm, from the Scandinavian *by* or *bey.* This name may have been applied to one who lived at the farm formerly occupied by the smith.

SMITHBONE—Variant of Smithburn, *q.v.*

SMITHBOUR—Variant of Smithbauer, *q.v.*

SMITHBROW—This is probably a shortened form of *borough,* a fortified place, and the smith who lived there was so named.

SMITHBURG—The surname here arose from one taking his name from Smithburg, that is, the Smith's town. The Old English *burg,* now written borough, meant a town, especially a fortified town or one with special privileges. The term was also applied to a manorhouse.

SMITHBURN—The smith who lived by the *burn,* an Anglo-Saxon word for a body of water such as a brook or stream.

SMITHBURNE—See Smithburn. The *e* was often added as a scribe's flourish.

SMITHCHESTER—This has an origin similar to Smithburg. *Chester,* now obsolete except in combinations, means a city or walled town, originally one that had been a Roman station in Britain. It is derived from the Latin *castra* and is one of the few Latin words adopted by the Angles and Saxons. The Old English form was *ceaster*.

SMITHCO—An Anglicization of the Teutonic *Smitko*, the little smith.

SMITHCONE—The smith who lived or had his smithy in the cove, a hollow or recess in a rock, a cave or cavern. The change from *cove* to *cone* was brought about for phonetic reasons.

SMITHCORS—The smith who lived by the market-place, known as a cross from the monument in the form of a cross often placed there for religious purposes. In the fifteenth and sixteenth centuries *cross* was spelled *cors*. The name may also refer to the smith's location near the cross, as crosses were often erected in other places of resort. The word is found today in many modern, English place-names due to this old religious practice.

SMITHDALE—The smith who lived in or near the dale, from the Anglo-Saxon *dahl*, meaning a meadow or valley.

SMITHDAS—Research has failed to disclose an explanation for this surname.

SMITHDEAL—Dweller in the Smith's valley, from Old English *dael,* a dale or valley.

SMITHDIEHL—This may be from the Anglo-Saxon *dahl,* meaning a meadow or valley, or it may indicate a woodsmith from the German *diele* meaning plank or floor.

SMITHE—An early spelling of Smith, now quite rare; this is also an early form of Smithy, *q.v.*

SMITHEA—The smith who lived by the water, from Old English *ea,* water or stream.

SMITHEAL—A contraction of Smithdeal, *q.v.*

SMITHEE—Variant of Smithies, *q.v.*

SMITHEIMER—Variant of Smithheimer, *q.v.*

SMITHEIS—A contraction of Smitheisen, *q.v.*

SMITHEISEN—A blacksmith or worker in iron, from the German *eisen* meaning iron.

SMITHEL—As a termination, the Anglo-Saxon *-eld* denotes persons, so Smithel would mean one who is a smith. See also Elsmith.

SMITHELLS—The Anglo-Saxon *-el* (see above) was sometimes written *-ell,* so this name would mean the son of a smith. Anglo-Saxon *ell* also means foreign, so the name might indicate the foreign smith. Also possibly local from Smithills in Lancashire, "the smooth hill."

SMITHEM—See Smitham.

SMITHEMAN—One who works at a smithy; the smith's assistant, probably an apprentice.

SMITHEN—Variant of Smithend, *q.v.*

SMITHENBANK—The smith on the bank or hillock, from the Anglo-Saxon *banc* meaning hillock. The Anglo-Saxon *-en* forms a masculine termination of nouns. The name may be of German origin as German *bank* has a meaning similar to the English word. The German *en* means in.

SMITHEND—The suffix *-end* in Anglo-Saxon denotes the agent, so Smithend means one who is a smith.

SMITHENDORF—The smith in the village, from the German *en* meaning in, and *dorf* meaning village.

SMITHEO—Variant of Smithea, *q.v.*

SMITHER—A smith, one who smiths. The Anglo-Saxon termination *-er* denotes a masculine occupation. As a word it is formed by the verb *smith* plus *er*. The ending is very common in trades, both early ones and modern ones, and designates the person who engages in that trade. Hundreds could be listed, but only a few examples will be given, as Builder, Dyer, Butler, Butcher, Slater, Tanner, Cutter, and Weaver. It also appears to mean light or active, as in the *Anturs of Arthur,*

> "Gawan was smyther and smerte,
> Owte of his sterroppus he sterte."

It is also a rare form for smith, formed by the verb *smith* plus *er*. Smither is a Lincolnshire word for a fragment. In provincial English it has a meaning of light rain. See also Smithies.

SMITHERAL—The foreign smith, from the Anglo-Saxon *el* meaning foreigner. The change from *e* to *a* is common. The Anglo-Saxon termination *-el* also denotes persons. See Smithel.

SMITHERAM—Dweller at the smith's home or enclosure, from the Anglo-Saxon *hám* meaning homestead or enclosure. See Smither.

SMITHERAN—Variant of Smithan, *q.v.* See also Smither.

SMITHERFIELD—Dweller at the smith's field; the smith who lived by the field or clearing. See Smither.

SMITHERIN—See Smither and Smithin.

SMITHERINGALE—This name has a meaning of "the smith settlement in the ravine or narrow lane" or "the smith's ravine." It is usually true that *ing* is a patronymic, but it occasionally has a topographic significance in Anglo-Saxon place-names. The suffix *-gale* denotes a ravine or narrow lane. It is the Scottish *gill* and the Old Norse *geil,* pronounced *gale.* The Anglo-Saxon *-ing* was sometimes used as the equivalent of the genitive or possessive, and used in this way the second meaning given above would be the correct one. The *er* in the name seems to be for phonetic reasons. See Smither.

SMITHERLIN—The smith who lived near a deep pool or lake, from the old English *lynn* with that meaning. See Smithlin and Smither.

SMITHERMAN—See Smitheman and Smither.

SMITHERN—Dweller at the smith's place, from the Anglo-Saxon *ern* meaning a place, or habitation. It has also been defined as a retired, melancholy spot, and would indicate the smith who lived near there.

SMITHERNS—See Smithern.

SMITHERON—The little smith, from *Smither, q.v.* plus *on.*

SMITHERS—This may be a corruption of Smethurst, *q.v.* The suffix *-house* is sometimes changed into *-ers* and thus the meaning may be the dweller in or near the smith's house. See Smither. Smithers is peculiar to Surrey in England.

SMITHERSON—The son of the smith. See Smither.

SMITHES—This is the early English genitive case ending, most usually found in the surnames of women. It is sometimes the feminine agential suffix *-ess.*

SMITHETT—One who came from Smurthwaite, *q.v.* But it might designate the little smith, as the suffix *-ett* indicates a diminutive; or the smith's clearing, from thwaite, a "clearing."

SMITHETTE—Same as Smithett, *q.v.*

SMITHEVICH—The "smith's son." This is the Slavic patronymical ending, *-evich,* which is usually found attached only to Christian names. The name was probably formed in this country by Russian immigrants who adopted an American name to which was added, either by themselves or their Russian friends, the Russian termination familiar to them.

SMITHEY—*Ey* (sometimes *ay*) represents *hey* or *hay,* the *h* being elided, and meant a hedge, an enclosed place; the dweller at the smith's enclosed place. Another meaning of *ey*—anciently written *ea*—is water, so this would indicate the smith who lived by the water. The early Danes in England used *ey* to mean an island, so in some cases it may refer to the smith who lived on an island. In some instances it is the same as Smithy, *q.v.*

SMITHFEL—The smith who lived by or on the *fel,* a Middle-English word, now obsolete, meaning hill or mountain. In the north of England it also meant a wild, elevated stretch of waste or pasture land; a moorland ridge, down.

SMITHFIELD—This is a modern perversion of *Smoothfield,* in London, an extensive tract of meadow land (in early times) where horses were sold and tournaments were held as far. back as the twelfth century. A horserace is recorded as witnessed in *Smoothfield* in the year 1154. Now a large market selling poultry, fish, vegetables, and hay, known as the London Central Meat Market, and under the control of the City Corporation, occupies this site. Seventeen villages and communities in the United States bear this name. As a surname it designates one who came from Smithfield. It may also designate the smith who lived by the field or clearing. It is found as early as the Hundred Rolls, where it was spelled Smethefeld and Smythefeld.

SMITHFOR—The man who lived by the way or approach to the smith's place, from the Anglo-Saxon *for* meaning course, way, approach.

SMITHFORDE—The person who lived near the ford by the smithy.

SMITHGALL—The smith who lived in the ravine. *Gall* is from the Anglo-Saxon, meaning ravine or narrow lane.

SMITHGARD—Dweller in or near the smith's dwelling, from the Old English *geard,* of which *gard* is a variant.

SMITHGRAY—The smith who lived near the thicket, from the Middle English *greve,* a thicket. There is a well-defined tendency for an obsolete syllable in a name to change into a common one.

SMITHGRUHNER—This seems to be from the German *grun* meaning green, the color. The name may be similar to Greensmith, *q.v.*

SMITHHAMMER—This is from the German *Schmidthamer,* signifying one who came from Schmidtham, a place in Germany.

SMITHHART—A smith "of heart or courage." The German *hart* means cruel, severe, hard, austere, and the name may refer to that quality in the smith. *Hart* is also the name of several woody districts in Germany.

SMITHHEART—Variant of Smithart, or of Smithhart, *q.v.*

SMITHHEIMER—A smith's home, from the German *heim* meaning home. As a surname it would designate one who lived in the home of a smith, who was probably not himself a smith. It may, however, be a variation of Smithhammer, *q.v.*

SMITHHEISLER—The fireman, or stoker, who helped the smith with the furnace, from the German *heizer* meaning firemaker, furnace-man or fireman.

SMITHHEURST—The smith who lived by the hurst or wood, from the Anglo-Saxon *hyrst*. *Hurst* is often found in place names, although it is rarely found by itself.

SMITHHISLER—Variant of Smithheisler, *q.v.*

SMITHI—An early spelling of Smithy, *q.v.* East Frisian *smithi* is the verb, to smith, that is, to forge, or fashion articles out of iron.

SMITHIARD—The man who worked at the smithy located on or near the *ard,* a Gaelic word for height or hill.

SMITHICK—Variant of Smithwick, *q.v.*

SMITHIE—Variant of Smithey, *q.v.*

SMITHIER—A smith. The word is now archaic and rarely found. It was formed by the verb *smithy* plus -*er,* or, in early use, by the verb *smith* plus -*ier.*

SMITHIERS—The son of Smith. See Smithier.

SMITHIES—Dweller at the smithy. One who came from Smethurst.

SMITHIGAL—Variant of Smythergill, *q.v.*

SMITHIJES—Variant of Smithies, *q.v.* See Smijth in Chapter 3.

SMITHILL—The smith on the hill.

SMITHILLE—Variant of Smithill, *q.v.*

SMITHIMAN—Variant of Smitheman, *q.v.*

SMITHIN—See Smithend. This may, however, be a diminutive form. The name here might mean the smith who lived by the common pasture or meadow from the word *ing* which had that meaning in the north of England. The *g* was often dropped in speech. See also the explanation given under Smitheringale.

SMITHINE—Variant of Smithlin, *q.v.*

SMITHING—The smith who lived by the *ing,* a word used in the north of England to mean a common pasture or meadow.

SMITHINGER—See Smithing. The termination -*er* is frequently added to designate one who lives by a topographical element, and means the same as "at the."

SMITHIS—The suffix -*is* is a frequent Middle English variant of the grammatical inflexion -*es, -s,* of the genitive singular, and the plural of substantives. The name may, however, be a diminutive form.

SMITHKA—The little smith. The diminutive ending -*ka* is either Finnish or German.

SMITHKE—From the German *Schmidtke,* meaning the little smith.

SMITHKEN—The little smith. The Low German diminutive ending -*ken* is a weakened form of -*kin.*

SMITHKEY—Variant of Smithke, *q.v.*

SMITHKIN—The little smith; the suffix -*kin* was found very early in England as a diminutive. The ending is generally found with a Christian name when used in a surname, but it can be used with common nouns to denote size.

SMITHKINS—Same as Smithkin, *q.v.*

SMITHKO—The little smith, from a Slavic diminutive ending.

SMITHKORS—Variant of Smithcors, *q.v.*

SMITHKOWSKI—The "son of the smith," from the Polish ending -*kowski,* meaning "son of". The surname was probably formed in the same way as the Russian Smithevich, *q.v.*

SMITHLAK—The smith who lived by the lake, often spelled *lak* in the fourteenth century. Besides the meaning we give to the word today, it included, in early England, a small stream.

SMITHLAND—One who lived on the land owned by the smith, or on land, for which rent was paid by smithwork.

SMITHLEIN—The little smith, from the High German diminutive ending *-lein.*

SMITHLEN—A variant of Smithlin, *q.v.*

SMITHLEY—The smith who lived by the *lagu,* Anglo-Saxon word for pool.

SMITHLIN—The smith who lived by a deep pool or lake from Old English *lynn* with that meaning. Of course *lin* is also a diminutive, but trade names with a diminutive are rare, and so another meaning must be sought whenever possible.

SMITHLINE—See Smithlin. The *e* was often added merely as a scribe's flourish.

SMITHLING—Same as Smithlin, *q.v.* with the excrescent *g.*

SMITHLOCK—The smith by the inlet, from the Gaelic *loch,* a fjord or inlet. It may also be the smith's enclosure, from Old English *loca.*

SMITHLOFF—From Slavic *ov,* a possessive form giving the sense of "Smith's." This surname is Slavicized by the suffix added.

SMITHMAN—One who works at a smithy. Also, the smith's assistant, probably an apprentice.

SMITHMEIER—Variant of Smithmeyer, *q.v.*

SMITHMEYER—Meyer is from the modern German *meier,* a bailiff, steward, farmer, mayor. Thus Smithmeyer indicates the smith who was the bailiff, etc. It may also be a double or hyphenated name run together.

SMITHMIER—Variant of Smithmeyer, *q.v.*

SMITHMIN—The man who lived in or near the smithy in which the work was partly performed by water power, from Middle English, *smethymylne* or *smithy-miln* (smith's mill).

SMITHNER—Dweller at or near the smith's refuge, from Old English *ner,* refuge or protection.

SMITHNIGHT—From the German *schmittknecht,* an obsolete word for a journeyman blacksmith, the worker in the black metal or iron.

SMITHOK—A condensed form of Smithlock, *q.v.*

SMITHOLM—This is the smith who lived in the *holm,* early English for the river-island.

SMITHON—The little smith.

SMITHOOVER—The smith who was also a small farmer, from the German *huber,* a small farmer.

SMITHORUDE—The smith at the clearning or open space in the forest.

SMITHOUSE—Dweller in or near the Smith-house. The suffix -*house* is quite common in surnames.

SMITHPETER—This is one of the few English surnames where a first name is added to Smith. It is in some cases a translation of a German name.

SMITHPETERS—Variant of Smithpeter, *q.v.*

SMITHREVISH—Variant of Smithevich, *q.v.*

SMITHREVITH—The smith's son. This is the Slavic patronymical ending -*evich* in which the *c* has dropped out. See Smithevich.

SMITHRICK—Variant of Smithridge, *q.v.*

SMITHRIDGE—The smith who lived by or on the ridge, a long hill or chain of hills.

SMITHROYD—A *royd* or *rode* was an old term implying a riding or clearing. It was often compounded with the personal name of the settler or occupant, but was sometimes compounded with his occupation as in this case.

SMITHRUD—Variant of Smithrude, *q.v.*

SMITHRUDE—One who lived by the smith's clearing, from Old English *ryden,* with that meaning.

SMITHS—A Gothic form of Smith. It may also be an English possessive form. See Smithson, also Smithis.

SMITHSBY—One who lived at the smith's habitation or farm, from the Scandinavian *by,* a farm dwelling.

SMITHSEN—Variant of Smithson, *q.v.* A Scandinavian form of son is *sen.*

SMITHSEND—The smith who lived at the end of the town, or one who lived on the smith's land which was located at the end of the town. When attempting to distinguish between two smiths, if one lived at the end of the town, it would be only natural to speak of him in this manner, hence the surname would thus arise easily.

SMITHSI—The workshop of a smith, from Dutch *Smidse*. See Smithy.

SMITHSLER—A contraction of Smithausler, *q.v.*

SMITHSOME—This is a variation of Smithsonne, an old spelling of Smithson.

SMITHSON—The Smith's son. One probably received the name Smithson rather than just Smith when he failed to follow the trade of his father, the smith, and went into something else, or perhaps went off to the wars. It may also be local of Smithstone in County Devon.

SMITHSONNE—An old spelling of Smithson, *q.v.*

SMITHSTAD—The smith in the city, from the Teutonic *stad,* city.

SMITHSTON—Variant of Smithstone, *q.v.* It may also be a variant of Smithson in some cases.

SMITHSTONE—One who came from Smithstone in County Devon; dweller near Smithstone.

SMITHT—An old Scottish spelling of Smith.

SMITHTANA—From the Slavic name *Smetana* which means, literally, sour cream. This is an instance of an unfamiliar foreign syllable changing into a familiar native syllable. In the Gaelic, *tana* means thin, or lean, so the name may refer to the smith's figure.

SMITHTATER—From the German *tater* meaning acts. It may, however, be from the German *tate,* a childish word for father, like dad, and thus designate father smith.

SMITHTON—The smith near the town or the enclosed space, from the Anglo-Saxon *tun,* signifying the enclosed plot of land, the area of which may be either large or small, from a cottage-homestead up to a walled town. The modern English *ton* is one of the most common endings of place-names and hence of local surnames.

SMITHTRO—The smith's town or enclosure, hence one who comes from the smith's town, from the Cornish *tre* meaning town or enclosure.

SMITHU—Dweller at or near the smithy(?).

SMITHURN—Variant of Smithburn, *q.v.*

SMITHURST—A corruption of Smethurst, *q.v.* Also a dweller at the smith's wood, from the Old English *hyrst,* a wood.

SMITHUS—A contraction of Smithouse, *q.v.* The termination *-us* from Old English *hus* (house) is found in many surnames.

SMITHUYSEN—One who lived in or near the smith's house, from Dutch *huysen,* house.

SMITHVILLE—From the Latin and French *villa*. This name designates the man who came from the smith's town.

SMITHWA—The last syllable in this name is probably the Slavic feminine termination *-ova,* and thus designates the female surnamed Smith.

SMITHWAITE—One who came from Smurthwaite, *q.v.* The first stage of corruption is Smuthwaite, the second, Smithwaite. Smithwaite may also be a corruption of Smiththwaite, the smith's clearing.

SMITHWECK—Variant of Smithwick, *q.v.*

SMITHWEEKE—Variant of Smithwick, *q.v.*

SMITHWHITE—This is a version of Smiththwaite, which means the smith's clearing. *Thwaite* is quite often changed to *white* in suffixes.

SMITHWICH—Variant of Smithwick, *q.v.*

SMITHWICK—Dweller at the smith's place. Also local of Smithwick, a township in the parish of Bereton, County Cheshire, four miles from Sandbach; also a hamlet in the parish of Harborne, County Stafford. The popular pronunciation was Smithick.

SMITHWICKE—Same as Smithwick, *q.v.*

SMITHWOOD—The smith who lived and had his forge in the wood. As almost every forest of any size in England surnamed a family, it is not surprising to find the word added to smith to distinguish one early metal-worker from another.

SMITHY—From the Anglo-Saxon smiththe, (smiþþe) a smithy, i.e. the workshop of a smith. The surname would thus come from working "at the smithy," and be a local surname. See also Smido. In various parts of England the phrase "to come past the smithy," means to have a sharp temper, but it is not likely that this meaning affected the meaning of the name. Smithy is also used colloquially to mean a low dirty place, a dwelling house, a home, a poor mean-looking place, and it is possible that a few families acquired their name from this fact.

SMITHYES—Variant of Smithies, *q.v.*

SMITHYMAN—Variant of Smithman, *q.v.* In *Isumbras* the word is spelled Smethymene and used to mean a smith, as the following quotation shows:
"Bot als the knyghte went thorow a lawe,
    Smethymene thore horde he blawe."
In the next verse the same word is spelled smethymane.

SMITHZERBERG—The smith at the castle, from German *zur burg.*

SMITKIEWICZ—The Low German form of Smith partly Slavicized by the addition of the Polish patronymical suffix *-wicz* (son).

SMITKO—The little smith. Teutonic form.

SMITKOSKI—A contraction of Smitkowski, *q.v.*

SMITKOWSKI—The "son of Smith," the Low German form plus the Polish patronymical suffix, formed by the German name being partly Slavicized.

SMITLAP—The Low German form plus Anglo-Saxon *laeppa,* a district, and thus refers to the smith's place.

SMITLEY—A Low German form. See Smithley.

SMITMAN—See Smit and Smithman.

SMITS—The son of Smit, *q.v.*

SMITSON—The son of Smit, *q.v.*

SMITT—Variant of Smit, *q.v.* The spelling with the two tt's is not as frequently found.

SMITTAN—Variant of Smyttan, *q.v.*

SMITTERS—See Smit and Smithers, *q.v.*

SMITTH—A curious early variation of the spelling of Smith found among the early settlers in this country, probably having its origin in a partial Anglicization of the German *Smitt.*

SMITTI—Variation of Smity, *q.v.*

SMITTON—One who came from Smitton, the smith's town. But see also Smeaton.

SMITTOUNE—An old Scottish form of Smithton, *q.v.*

SMITTY—This is a modern derivation of Smith, originated by the common practice of giving the nickname of Smitty to persons surnamed Smith. It is also a variation of Smithy, and thus denotes one who worked at the smithy.

SMITY—A surname found in the early part of the seventeenth century, probably a variant of Smithy, *q.v.*

SMITZ—A Low German form of Smith.

SMITZER—The Low German Smitz with the analogical suffix *er* added.

SMITZIN—The Low German form plus the Slavic possessive suffix *-in*, giving the meaning of "Smith's."

SMIZ—An early spelling of Smith (1250).

SMORTHWAITE—One who came down from Smurthwaite, one of the many localities in Cumberland, Westmorland and North Lancashire counties whose suffic is *-thwaite*, meaning clearing, the first element probably meaning small.

SMUT—This is said to be a corruption of Smith, but this theory seems doubtful.

SMUTH—A·miner's name for poor, small coal. It may thus have been applied in a derogatory manner to an inefficient smith. It is more likely, however, that the surname came through a corruption in spelling, or it may be merely an undotted double *i*. In the fourteenth century smooth was sometimes spelled in this way.

SMUTHERS—Variant of Smithers, *q.v.*

SMYDTHE—Early form of Smithy, which was spelled Smyththe. See Smidth.

SMYGHT—A curious early spelling of Smith, found in the Poll Tax list of the West Riding of Yorkshire made in 1379, as well as in the Early Chancery Proceedings (1385-1467) published by The Harleian Society, Volume 79, London, 1928. As a word, *smight* is an obsolete form of the verb, *smite,* and the name here was probably pronounced smite.

SMYITH—An early Scottish variation.

SMYITHE—An early Scottish form.

SMYTH—An old orthography of Smith. See Chapter 3.

SMYTHBERD—One with ·a smooth beard. A Scottish corruption of *smeth berd,* i.e. smooth beard.

SMYTHE—Variation of Smyth. See Chapter 3.

SMYTHENATON—The smith in the *tun* or farm, an old Devonshire form.

SMYTHENEHEIE—Variation of Smythsheies, *q.v.*

SMYTHEOT—The smith who came from Jutland, from the Anglo-

Saxon *Eota,* Jute. This name may also be a diminutive form as both *et* and *ot* are diminutives.

SMYTHERGILL—The smith who lived in the ravine, from the Scottish *gill,* ravine.

SMYTHERS—Variant of Smithers, *q.v.*

SMYTHES—A genitive form of Smith. See Smithes.

SMYTHESSONE—An early spelling of Smithson, *q.v.*

SMYTHESTON—The person from the smith's *tun* or farm.

SMYTHHUSEN—One who was a member of the smith's family, or who lived in the house of the smith, from the Anglo-Saxon *hus* meaning house or family. The suffix *-en* is often added to Anglo-Saxon nouns.

SMYTHIA—See Smido.

SMYTHIES—An old spelling of Smithies, *q.v.*

SMYTHSHEIES—The person who lived in or near the smith's enclosure from *heghe* or *hey,* the hedge or enclosure, an early surname found in Devonshire.

SMYTHSONN—An old spelling of Smithson, *q.v.*

SMYTHY—Variant of Smitht, *q.v.*

SMYTHWINE—The smith who was a friend or protector, from Old English *wine,* a common element in English and German names.

SMYTHWYT—The smith of understanding or learning, from the Anglo-Saxon *wita.*

SMYTHY—Variant of Smithy, *q.v.*

SMYTTAN—An Old English form of Smith. The word however seems to be from the Anglo-Saxon *smitan,* and this may be an instance where a man earned his name because of his "smiting the anvil," the name in its origin thus being entirely distinct from Smith.

SMYTTHE—A fourteenth century spelling of Smithy, *q.v.*

SNESMYTH—This name designates one who lived by the smith's clearing or woodland, from Old English *snaed.*

SOCKSMITH—The smith who made "socks," an old word in the north of England for the plough-share.

SONSMITH—The smith who lived near the sand or sandbank, from Old English *sond.* It may, however, be from Old English *sund,* watercourse or sea, and thus designate the smith who worked nearby.

SOOYSMITH—This is a combination of the surname *Sooy* with that of *Smith.* It was first run together by Charles Sooysmith who died in 1916, a son of William Sooy Smith. It is also found with the second *S* capitalized.

SOSMYTH—An early form of Shoesmith, *q.v.*

SPEARSMITH—The smith who made spears. The word is derived from the Anglo-Saxon *spere* used both for hurling and thrusting.

STAHLSMITH—From the German *Stahlschmidt,* which is translated to mean a worker in steel. See Steelsmith.

STALLSMITH—A variation of Stahlsmith, *q.v.*

STALSMITH—A variation of Stahlsmith, *q.v.*

STEELSMITH—As all smiths wrought steel, to some extent at least, this name must have been given to one who specialized in steel work. Steel is just a name for iron more nearly chemically pure than other iron, and is distinguished from the substance known as iron by its greater hardness and elasticity. Thus all smiths who made swords or cutting tools of any kind would use the best iron available for the purpose, which would be steel. The English name may be a translation of the German *Stahlsmith.*

SUCKSMITH—*Suck* is a sixteenth century spelling for *sock.* See Socksmith. It may also be one of the many variations of Shoesmith, *q.v.* It has also been suggested that it is a corruption of Sixsmith, *q.v.*

SUESMITH—Corruption of Shoesmith, be one of the many variations of Shoesmith, *q.v.* It has also been suggested that it is a corruption of Sixsmith, *q.v.*

SUESMITH—Corruption of Shoesmith, *q.v.*

SUGHSMYTH—Corruption of Shoesmith, *q.v.*

SUKSMYTHE—Variant of Sucksmith, *q.v.*

SUSMITH—A contraction of south smith. When several smiths lived in one small village they might easily be referred to according to the direction they lived from the center of the village. In some cases it may be one of the many variations found of Shoesmith, from the early English spelling *sue.*

SYKELSMITH—Variant of Sicklesmith, *q.v.*

TELSMITH—The smith who made tile, from Middle English *tile.*

However, it may be the smith who used the German *tellerhammer*, a flattening hammer.

TEXSMITH—This is from Old English þiox meaning a hunting spear, and the name here designates the smith who made them. Also a corruption of the German Tuchschmidt, the cloth weaver.

THOOSMITH—Possibly the thunder-smith, from Old English ðunor, a name applied, perhaps, to a noisy smith.

TINSMITH—The smith who worked with tin. This name is quite rare. There is only one in the New York City directory. It is found more frequently in its German form, *Blechschmidt*.

TROWSMITH—One who worked with wood, a woodsmith or carpenter.

ULLSMITH—The smith who made pottery. Variant of Wolfsmith, *q.v.*

VANDERSMITH—Vander is the Dutch form, and means "of the smith." The name here is partially Anglicized.

VON SMITH—This is probably from the German Von Schmidt. When a man was ennobled in Germany, *von* was prefixed to his name.

VONDERSMITH—A Dutch form. See Vandersmith.

WACHSMITH—One who worked with wax; the smith who stood guard.

WAFFENSMITH—The smith who made weapons, from the German *waffe* (old form *waffen*) meaning weapon. This term would include a gunsmith.

WAINSMITH—The smith who made wagons.

WALBSMITH—The smith in the forest, from Old English *wald*. See Waldsmith.

WALDSMITH—From the German *Waldschmidt*. The German and Old English *wald* means forest, and it was only natural for the many smiths who worked in the forest, in order to have ample fuel for their fires near at hand, to be called Waldsmith to distinguish them from the smiths in the town.

WALSMITH—Variant of Waldsmith, *q.v.* The word *wal,* from the Anglo-Saxon *wealh,* also has a meaning of stranger or foreigner, and the name may thus designate the foreign smith.

WATERSMITH—Probably indicates a smith who lived near a large pond or river. It might be the same as the waterleder, a laborer who led the water into furrows or drains, being what we would now call a drainer. It has also been suggested that this is a smith who used a hammer driven by water.

WAYNESMITH—The smith who made wagons, from Middle English *wayne,* wagon.

WELSMYTH—An early spelling of Whelsmyth, *q.v.* In some instances it might be a variation of Walsmith or Wildsmith, *q.v.*

WESTSMITH—A smith might be so named from his position with regard to another smith; the smith in the western part of the village.

WHELSMYTH—The smith who made wheels, especially the iron parts, from Old English, *hwēol* meaning wheel.

WHILESMITH—A corruption of Wildsmith, *q.v.*

WHITESMITH—The smith who worked in tin. The name is from the occupation "white ironsmith," or "white-iron men" as they were sometimes known. The name is also applied to a worker in iron who finishes or polishes the work in contrast to one who forges it.

WIGSMITH—Bosworth-Toller's Anglo-Saxon Dictionary says a *wig-smiþ* is an idol-smith or maker of idols, and the name is probably derived from that. *Wig-smiþ* is also a war-smith, or warrior, as used in the *Anglo-Saxon Chronicle* (see Chapter 1), but this is a poetical compound and probably did not influence the surname in any way.

WILDSMITH—The forest smith, from the Anglo-Saxon *weald* meaning forest. As an early English form of this word was *wild,* the spelling of the surname in this manner is not surprising. In some instances the surname may be a variation of the German *Waldschmidt,* having the same meaning, from *wald,* a forest. As in early times the smith used wood and not coal in his forge, his location near a forest was almost a necessity. It was easier to bring the ore to the forest, than to take the wood to the ore. It has been suggested that the name is a corruption of weldsmith, but this is unlikely as is also the view that it refers to a personal characteristic.

WILESMITH—Variant of Wildsmith, *q.v.*

WILLDSMITHE—An old form of Wildsmith, *q.v.*

WINTERSMITH—A smith who worked in a different place in the winter. An archaic meaning of the word is an implement made to hang on a grate for the purposes of keeping a kettle warm, and this name would be applied to the smith who made them. Winter is also an Anglo-Saxon personal name.

WIRESMYTH—The smith who made wire, a wiredrawer.

WOBENSMITH—This is a German compound meaning the weaver, from the German *weben*. James C. Wobensmith says that there is a legend in his family to the effect that at the time that names were being adopted, one of the progenitors was a seal maker for one of the petty German kings. Some others insist that it is a corruption of Waffenschmidt, or weapon-smith.

WOLFSMITH—This is from the German *Wolfschmidt*. While the German *wolf* has the same meaning as the word does in English, it has another meaning in German from which the name is derived in the present instance. It may be defined as a lump of malleable iron obtained directly from the furnace. A *wolfschmiede* is a smith employed in the smelting works of a mine. Thus the name refers to the smith who worked with iron as it came from the furnace.

WOLLESMITH—Probably an early erratic orthography of Wildsmith, *q.v.* It may, in some cases, designate a worker with wool from the German word *wolle* meaning wool.

WOODSMITH—The smith who worked in wood. It would seem that this would have the same meaning as wright, and if so, must have originated before wright and smith came to have separate meanings. The name might designate the smith in the forest or wood or it might be "the mad smith," from Anglo-Saxon *woda* "madman."

WRIGHTSMITH—This seems to be a strange compound since in early times *wright* and *smith* were identical. Later *smith* was used to mean those who worked in metals and *wright* in wood and other materials. The name might have the same meaning as Woodsmith. The name may have originated from some combination of the two trades by one man. Again, in early times the word *smith* might have been added to explain the word *wright*, which at that time was a descriptive word rather than a hereditary family name.

WURTSMITH—The smith who planted herbs or kept a garden, from Anglo-Saxon *wyrt* meaning herb or root, especially a garden herb.

YONGSMITH—Variant of Youngsmith, *q.v.*

YOUNGESMITHE—An early form of Youngsmith, *q.v.*

YOUNGSMITH—From the nickname, "the young smith." While the name was quite common in the early records it is quite rare in modern times. Most have now contracted their name to Young, which is a very common surname. We have a corresponding Oldsmith, *q.v.*, and also the name Aldersmith, *q.v.* Ordinarily when one attains such an age as to receive a nickname referring to it, he is not likely to be able to carry on such arduous work as the smith is required to do. The older Smith would have received his surname in most cases before he had a son or a younger smith working with him, and when such an event did happen, it would not cause his surname to be changed. Instead the younger man would receive a designation to distinguish him from the elder smith.

ZILVERSMIT—Dutch form of Silversmith, *q.v.*

ZUGSMITH—From the German *Zugschmidt,* the smith who worked with fibrous iron.

NOTE TO GLOSSARY OF SMITH COMPOUNDS

In Germany, compounds with Schmidt are quite common as surnames, much more so than in England. Many Germans have in the past, and will in the future, translate their names into English. The following is a list of German combinations with a translation or explanation of the German prefix. If after translation the name was found in English or American directories, it has been included in the main part of this chapter.

A curious German practice, which is seldom found in England or America, is the use of Schmidt as a prefix to a first name to form a surname, as Schmitthenner (Henry), Schmitjan (John), Schmidtkunz (Conrad), and Schmidtseifert (Siegfried).

France does not compound the name Smith, except perhaps in Orfevre (Goldsmith). French Smiths take distinctive names as a rule, for example, Chaudelier (Coppersmith), Serruel (Locksmith), Armorier (Gunsmith), and Taillandier (Blacksmith).

German Compounds	*Translation or Explanation*
Bachschmidt	brook
Bartschmidt	beard
Bauernschmidt	peasant
Bauerschmidt	peasant
Bayerschmidt	Bavarian
Behrschmidt	bear
Beilschmidt	hatchet
Bergschmidt	mountain
Blechschmidt	tin
Blumenschmid	flowers
Boberschmidt	Bober (river)
Breitschmid	broad
Broeksmit	crumble
Brueggenschmidt	bridge
Dorfschmidt	hamlet
Drahtschmidt	wire or woven coats of mail
Durschmidt	sharp
Eisenschmidt	iron
Feilschmidt	file
Freischmidt	free (outside of guild)
Gassenschmidt	lane
Goldschmidt	gold
Grobschmidt	rough work
Gutschmidt	good

German Compounds	*Translation or Explanation*
Hackenschmidt	hoe
Hammerschmidt	hammer
Haubenschmidt	steel hoods or caps worn in Middle Ages
Heitschmidt	heating block
Helmsmit	warrior's helmet
Hubschmidt	hide (of land)
Huffschmidt	horseshoe
Hufschmidt	horseshoe
Hugenschmidt	hill
Huobschmid	hide (of land)
Huttenschmid	foundry, hut
Isenschmid	iron
Jaegerschmidt	hunter
Kaltschmidt	cold (brazier who worked without fire)
Kleinschmidt	small
Klingelschmidt	bell
Klingenschmid	blade
Kopperschmidt	copper
Kuperschmidt	copper
Kupferschmidt	copper
Kupperschmied	copper
Lindenschmidt	linden
Loffelschmid	spoon
Messerschmidt	knife
Musterschmidt	pattern or die
Nagleschmidt	nail
Pfannenschmidt	pan
Pfannschmidt	pan
Pfeilschmidt	arrow
Pfennigschmidt	penny (maker of pennies?)
Phannenschmidt	pan
Psanuenschmid	pan
Pusterschmidt	bellows
Reinschmidt	Rhine

German Compounds	Translation or Explanation
Rheinschmidt	Rhine
Rosenschmidt	rose (at the sign of the rose)
Rotschmid	red (copper)
Schaarschmidt	plough-share
Scheerschmidt	shears
Schellenschmidt	bell
Schellschmidt	bell
Segenschmid	scythe
Seigerschmidt	watch or clock
Sensenschmidt	scythe
Sichelschmidt	sickle
Silberschmidt	silver
Sonnenschmidt	sun (near an inn at the sign of the sun)
Stahlschmidt	steel
Stuckenschmidt	tree stump
Thorschmidt	city gate
Thratschmid	dialectic variant of Drahtschmidt
Tuchschmidt	cloth
Waffenschmidt	arms or weapons
Waldschmidt	forest
Werschmidt	armor
Wolfschmitt	wolf
Wurschmidt	sausage
Wurstschmid	sausage
Zainschmid	small bar of metal
Zieglschmid	brick
Zugschmidt	fibrous iron

In German, as in English, there are also many other words compounded with smith which have not been found as surnames. Such words are: ankerschmidt (anchor); buchsenschmidt (gun); fahnenschmidt (flag; smith attached to cavalry); kettenschmidt (chains); messingschmidt (brass); and zirkelschmidt (compasses).